THE GOLD SEEKERS

Mark Young, ex-captain of the Confederate Army, agrees to guide a wagon train across the wastes to the goldfields of California. However, the wagon boss, Walt Shaw, begins to hate Young and his obvious attraction to pretty Shelia Blake. Discord and rivalry between the two men hamper the train's progress. But worse is to come: Indian attack, water shortages, and a desperate struggle to cross the hostile, mountainous terrain in time to beat the encroaching winter . . .

Books by E. C. Tubb
in the Linford Western Library:

THE FIRST SHOT

E. C. TUBB

THE GOLD SEEKERS

Complete and Unabridged

LINFORD
Leicester

First published in Great Britain in 2000

Originally published in paperback as
The Fighting Fury by Paul Schofield

First Linford Edition
published 2007

The moral right of the author has been asserted

All characters in this story are entirely imaginary,
and have no connection with, or reference to,
any living person.

British Library CIP Data

Tubb, E.C.
    The gold seekers.—Large print ed.—
Linford western library
1. Western stories
2. Large type books
I. Title II. Schofield, Paul. Fighting fury
823.9'14 [F]

ISBN 978–1–84617–588–6

Published by
F. A. Thorpe (Publishing)
Anstey, Leicestershire

Set by Words & Graphics Ltd.
Anstey, Leicestershire
Printed and bound in Great Britain by
T. J. International Ltd., Padstow, Cornwall

This book is printed on acid-free paper

1

A tall, spare, dark-haired man stood leaning against the bar in a saloon in Freeguard, the south-eastern gateway to the new lands of the West. He was dressed in buckskins, worn and rubbed with long usage, and a wide leather belt around his narrow waist supported a bone-handled Colt revolver and a heavy hunting knife. Cartridges studded the belt, and the holster was of the type known as a 'greaser' holster, one swivelled on the belt and with the bottom cut away so that it was possible to shoot without lifting the gun from the holster at all. He drank raw whisky with an absent carelessness, letting the potent spirit trickle down his throat as though it had been water, but as he drank, his cold, slate-grey eyes never left the long mirror at the back of the bar.

He stood like an island in a sea of noise. Around him men shouted, jostled each other, laughed and roared snatches of song. Even though it was still day, with the sun almost an hour from dusk, yet the two roulette wheels and faro table were in full swing. A piano, a gaudy thing imported by river steamer and wagon train from New Orleans, filled what gaps in the silence the red-faced men left open.

The bartender, a short, pale man, watched him anxiously. He looked at him, then at another man a few feet down the bar.

'Let's have no trouble,' the bartender said. 'Look, fellows, let's have no trouble in here. Have a drink. The drinks are on the house.'

'There'll be no trouble,' said the tall man. His eyes never left the reflected image of the man down the bar.

'Glad to hear it,' said the bartender. 'How about you, Fred?'

'I told you to keep your stinking nose

out of my business,' said Fred danger-ously. He was a thick, bearded man with pale eyes and slightly bowed legs. He wore two guns.

'Take no notice of him, Mark,' said the bartender hastily. 'You know Fred, he talks too much.'

'Far too much,' agreed the tall man. He lit a long thin cigar and blew smoke towards the bartender. 'Where's the free drink?'

Around them, drawn somehow by their attitudes or by that intangible something which tells men when other men are spoiling for a fight, several men formed a ring. The bartender sweated as he saw them.

'Break it up, fellows,' he said. 'Have a drink. Drinks on the house.'

'Watch him, Mark,' said an old, bowed man with a tobacco-stained beard. 'Fred's Fast.'

'Keep your nose out of this, Shorty,' snapped Fred. He glared at the tall man. 'What's all this talk about you warning the settlers from my store?'

'No talk.' Mark sipped at his whisky then turned so that he now looked at the man and not at his reflected image in the bar mirror. 'I'm sick of seeing what you've done out there. Bad flour, spoiled grain, dud cartridges. All sold at top prices and more. And the Indians, you cheat them at every turn and then they get sore and take it out on the wagon trains.'

'You setting yourself up as the law around here?' Fred spat. 'What the hell does a few Indians matter?'

'Plenty, to the people who lose their scalps to them.' Mark set down his glass. 'You're a trader, you say, but I know better. You got hold of ex-war stores, condemned as unfit for the forts, and you're selling them to the wagon trains. This is the last stop before California and there's a trail of bones from here to there caused by you and those like you.' He paused. 'You'd be better off dead.'

'Maybe you'd like to be the one to do it?' said Fred dangerously. He turned to the circle of men around them.

'You know me and you know I'm fair. Hell, are you going to let a no-good reb insult the town like that? You all know Mark, but what you don't know was that he wasn't always an Indian fighter. I knew him back in the old days. Captain Mark Young, he was then. Captain Young of Quantrell's raiders. Need I say More?'

He had said enough. The memory of the just-ended Civil War was too fresh for anyone to ever forget the notorious Quantrell and his band of raiders who had harried the North long after the war was supposed to have been over. Starting as patriots, they had fought behind the lines in a desperate effort to restore the balance of the war in the favour of the South. Later, as the desire for loot had overridden the original patriotism, their atrocities had revolted North and South alike in a union of common hatred.

'I was never with Quantrell,' said Mark evenly. 'Were you?'

'Why, you stinking no-good Indian lover,' snarled Fred. 'You ain't fit to be around decent people.'

The bartender whitened and the group of men moved hastily away. Mark shook his head.

'Seems to me that you've been talking like that before, Fred. Seems kind of hard to believe, but now you've come right out in the open with it and said it to my face. Seems like there's only one kind of answer to talk like that.'

Fred moved, his hands darted down towards the guns at his hips. Mark moved too, slightly, his hand dropping and his weapon exploding as he triggered it while still in the holster. Fred staggered, looked foolish, then crumpled in a lifeless heap. Mark stared down at him, then looked at the men around him.

'Anyone care to take up where he left off?' he asked mildly. The old man with the tobacco-stained beard spat a thin brown stream towards the dead man and shrugged.

'Hell, no, Mark. I reckoned he asked for it and he got it. You figuring to stay in town?'

'Maybe? Why?'

'Fred had friends. He was a member of the trading ring which he organised to cheat the settlers. You stick around and you'll end up with a knife in the back.' He looked apologetic. 'None of my business, I know, but I've seen it happen before.'

'I'll watch it,' said Mark. He stepped towards the door of the saloon, then paused as a man called to him from a table by the door. Two men sat there. One of them rose.

'Mr Young, will you join us in a drink?'

Mark hesitated, looking at them. Both were elderly men, bearded, wearing the thick trousers, high boots, and leather jackets of wagon handlers.

He nodded. 'Why not? Whisky.'

'We heard the argument at the bar,' said the man who had called to him. 'My name is Henderson and this is Carl

Blake. We are members of a wagon train leaving at dawn for California.' He paused. 'I'll be frank with you, Mr Young, neither of us has had much experience in this territory. From what I gather, you have. I'd take it kindly if you'd give us a little advice.'

'The name is Mark,' said the tall man. He grinned at the one called Carl. 'You want advice? Simple. Don't go.'

'We must go,' said Henderson. 'The members of our train have sold all they possess and carry all they own. We've got to find new lands to settle and we've got to do it soon.' He made a helpless gesture. 'We've had nothing but trouble ever since we started, and the people are losing heart. I'm afraid that they may begin to break away unless we make a move. That is why we are starting at dawn.'

'Where are you heading?'

'California.'

'The goldfields?' Mark sipped at his drink. 'That's a tough route right through Indian territory. You well-armed?'

'Yes.'

'Good. How many wagons?'

'Fifteen.'

'Families?'

'Fifteen of course, and we have the young men mounted on horses for outriders and scouts.'

'Then where's your trouble?' Mark leaned back in his chair. 'With fifteen good wagons and plenty of men well-armed I don't see that I can help you much. All you need is a guide, and there are enough of those around. Plenty of other wagon trains leave with a lot less than what you've got.'

Henderson looked at the man he had called Carl, and Carl looked back. He nodded.

'It just isn't as simple as that, Mark,' said Henderson. 'Originally we started out with the idea of finding farmlands and settling down. There's some good country out there just waiting to be developed. Then the news of the gold

9

strike came and immediately most of us wanted to rush off to the fields and stake a claim. The young men, mostly, but a number of the others agreed. So we changed direction and came here. Now, with all our money spent, we are afraid that we may be heading into something we don't know about.'

'Seems natural enough to me,' said Mark. 'What do you want me to do?'

'Can you tell us the best route? How to avoid the Indians? Where the waterholes are? Things like that.'

'Hire a guide,' said Mark shortly. He looked at the two men. 'What's the real trouble?'

'We've a young man called Walt Shaw,' said Blake. 'He isn't the wagon leader yet, but he will be soon unless someone stops him. He's crazy to get on at full speed and reach the goldfields early before the others do. He's managed to persuade the others to support him, but, Mark, the wagons won't stand it. The oxen too are near beat, we've come a long way, and if we left things to Walt we'd wind up lost or scalped, or worse.'

'Then change your wagon boss.'

'I am the wagon boss,' said Carl. 'But I'm not fooling myself. I'm not as young as I was and I'm no hand with a gun. If it came to a showdown, Walt will take over, for sure.'

'Then let him, what's the grief about?'

'You know the country, Mark. What chance has a disorganised wagon train of getting through?'

'Depends on what you mean by 'disorganised'. First there's the desert, that's bad enough on its own. You've got to carry plenty of water to cross it. Then there are the Indians, plenty of them, and then you hit the foothills and mountains. There's a trail of sorts and a few forts scattered around with trading posts and such. You can do it with luck and guts and judgment, but you'd be a lot better if you swung north to Thorneville and took the California route from there. This may be shorter, but it's much harder.'

'They won't turn north,' said Henderson grimly. He looked at Mark. 'What we're trying to do is to offer you a job. We need a man like you to act as guide and scout. Will you take it?'

'For how much?'

'We haven't much money, but we'll pay you all we've got. One thousand dollars. Is it a deal?'

'It's tempting.' Mark finished his drink and stood up. 'But not for me. I've only just arrived in town and I want to stay awhile. Sorry.'

'Wait.' Carl rose and stood beside him. 'Look. We're camped on the north edge of town about half a mile out. If you should change your mind you know where to find us. The offer still holds.'

'Find yourself a good scout,' snapped Mark. 'I've given you my answer.'

'We shall move at dawn and head for Fort Deacon. I understand that the first stage isn't too difficult. If you change your mind and decide to join us you'll be very welcome.' Carl held out his hand. 'Thanks for the advice, anyway.'

'Forget it.' Mark took the proffered hand. 'Don't forget to take plenty of water.'

He stepped out of the saloon and on to the boardwalk. Before him Freeguard stretched like some ugly growth on the fringe of the desert. There were no paved streets or sidewalks in Freeguard. Only the uneven boardwalks before the few shops and trading posts. There was no drainage of any kind, and pools of stagnant water and collected garbage were everywhere.

There was no single water supply and no river. Wells were dug anywhere and everywhere and water drawn from them until they filled with alkali and then the wells were abandoned without being filled in or boarded over. There were no lamps to light the streets at night and no semblance of law aside that which a man carried on his own belt.

There were a dozen saloons, and all of them did a twenty-four-hour trade. There were gunsmiths and harness stores, trading posts and feed depots. There was a Western-Union stage station and several farriers. There were a few restaurants and a couple of tailors and, over everything, sweltering in the hot sun, dust lay as thick as a shroud.

To a man used to the open freedom of the hills and desert Freeguard was a prison of the worst kind.

Mark stared at it, his nostrils wrinkling as the faint wind carried the stench of refuse. Stepping carefully he walked over to one of the restaurants, probably the cleanest place in Freeguard, and sat down at a table. A woman, grey-haired, wrinkled, and yet with a hardness belying her apparent age, stared towards him, then came forward, wiping her hands on her apron.

'Mark! Why didn't you let me know you were in town?'

'Hello, Mrs Murphy.' He smiled towards her. 'What's good to eat?'

'Everything's good to eat.' She raised her voice and called towards the kichen at the rear. 'Lopez! Fix a steak and trimmings for Captain Young and fix it quick.' She sat in a chair opposite him and her eyes softened as she stared at his lined features. 'How long you staying, Mark?'

'I don't know.' He stretched luxuriously. 'A few days, maybe more. How's Susan?'

'Well.' She fumbled in a pocket of her apron. 'I had a letter from her only last week. Sam's got a raise and his firm is talking about a partnership. The two children are fighting fit and everything's all right.' Something in his face made her put away the letter. 'They're all right, Mark,' she repeated. 'Nothing is going to hurt them now.'

'I hope not,' he said sombrely, then smiled at her. 'Anything good to go with that steak?'

'I'll get it.' She rose and left and he stared around the little restaurant.

Apart from himself it was deserted now, though earlier it had done a good trade from the wagon-drivers, hustlers, women shoppers loading up with the things they would need on the long trail to the West. Mrs Murphy, prematurely aged like most of the frontier women, had built and run the place almost single-handed ever since her arrival from Georgia a few years ago. Mark had helped her then, had watched while her son, Sam, had courted his sister, Susan, and had seen them return to the East where Sam had been offered a good job. He had been glad to see them go. The long, dragging years of the Civil War had done enough to them and they had earned the chance to live in peace.

Mrs Murphy could have returned with them, but she, like Mark, had decided to stay and help push the frontier back and back until it met the thriving settlements on the West Coast.

He looked up as she returned with a slender-necked bottle of wine.

'Here, Mark, I've saved it for you.' She polished a glass and set it before him. 'I bought a few cases from a man who passed through here. He decided that it would be better to carry water rather than wine to the goldfields. A wise choice.'

'Very wise,' said Mark. He sipped at the wine. 'How's trade?'

'Couldn't be better. If things go on at this rate, I'll be retiring soon.'

They both laughed. Both knew that she would never retire. Mark sobered as he stared at his wine.

'The news of the new diggings has certainly stirred things up,' he said. 'On the way in I passed at least three wagon trains heading for the mountains. They came up from Masilla but this seems to be the new stepping-off place. Better open a new wing, Mrs Murphy, you're going to need more room.'

'I'm doing all right as things are,' she said. 'If I grow any bigger I may start to get greedy, and then someone else'll start up and take my trade.' She looked sharply at Mark. 'Heard you had some trouble in the saloon.'

'Some,' he admitted. 'That steak ready yet?'

'I heard that you shot Fred, the trader.'

'Well?'

'He had it coming to him,' she said. 'I'm not denying that, but he wasn't alone, Mark, and the others'll get you for sure unless you leave town for a spell.'

'So Shorty told me.' He described the man with the tobacco-stained beard and she nodded.

'Shorty Manegin. He used to own the feed store until Fred won it from him in a poker game. Used to sell good measure too.'

'What I can't understand,' said Mark, frowning, 'is why the townsfolk allowed Fred to get away with what he did. How come no one ever tried to stop him before?'

'Fred was smart. He sold good stuff to the locals and saved the bad grain and feed for the wagon trains. By the time they found out that they'd been cheated they were too far out to complain. Fred fixed the other traders into a ring so that none of them would undercut each other's prices.' She dropped her voice. 'He was doing other things too.'

'I know,' he said shortly. 'Whisky and rifles to the Indians.' He shrugged. 'Well, no harm in their having Winchesters, I suppose, but a drunken Indian is a bad Indian. Bad to himself and to everyone he meets.' He looked up as a Mexican boy pushed open the kitchen door and came towards him with a platter bearing an inch-thick steak piled high with fried potatoes and fresh greens. He looked at them, then at Mrs Murphy.

'I get them from a couple of farmers who's started a truck garden a few miles from here,' she explained. 'I tell you, Mark, Freeguard is growing up. Wouldn't surprise me if we had a marshal the next time you call in, goodness knows we need one bad enough.'

He nodded, his mouth full of steak.

'Seems to me,' she went on, 'that we could do a lot worse than pick a man like you to tote the star. How about it, Mark? Would you be interested if the proposition was put to you?'

'No.'

'Well, maybe you're right,' she said, not the least discomfited by his curt refusal. 'It takes a lot of guts to clean up a town this size, guts and time, and there ain't much money in it either. All we can offer is the chance to die wearing a star. Don't seem much when you come down to it. 'Course, the kids and women and decent livers who get killed and poisoned by the filth don't really matter. They can't pay much either.'

'Stop it, Mrs Murphy.' Mark set down his fork and stared at her. 'You asked and I answered, no need to give me the works. I don't live here, anyway, and it seems to me that those that do should be willing to clean up their own mess.'

'Fair enough, Mark.' She was still quite calm. 'I told you that it was just a thought. You intend leaving soon?'

'No.'

'I'd think about it if I were you, Mark. Fred had friends, like I told you, and they may not take kindly to you shooting him the way you did.' She stared out of the window. 'Plenty of wagon trains pulling out and they all need a good guide and scout. They really need help, those people. They are setting out towards the West with no idea of what lies before them. Seems only neighbourly to give them a hand. Might earn a little money doing it too. Maybe you could even strike it rich out in California.'

'No.' He looked at her, the fork poised in his hand. 'Look, Mrs Murphy, you mean well, I know, but you're treading close to what doesn't concern you. Maybe we'd better just stop talking now? Or maybe you'd rather I ate somewhere else?'

'No need to talk like that, Mark.' Two

spots of colour burned in her sallow cheeks. 'You know that you're just like a son to me now that Sam's gone East. I don't like to see a good man waste himself among the Indians and maybe getting himself shot in some saloon. This is a big country, Mark, and we've all got to do something to build it up. If we don't then others will, and then we can't complain if we don't like the way they've done things. Like Fred. He tried in his own way, a bad way, but he tried. We've all got to try, Mark.' She dabbed at her eyes. 'I guess that's all I've got to say.'

He didn't answer, but, after he had eaten his meal, sat for a long time over the wine. He stared out of the windows to where the sky was darkening as the sun lowered itself beneath the horizon and dusk rapidly grew into night.

It was quite dark by the time he left.

2

If the saloons were crowded during the day, they were even more so at night. Men thronged the long bars and clustered around the faro and poker tables. Red-faced men, big, their shirts stained with sweat and their breath heavy with rot-gut liquor. Most of them carried guns, long-barrelled Colts, and all of them sported knives. Hard they were, ruthless in their fashion, but beneath the hardness and ruthlessness was the driving restlessness which had picked them up from their homes and driven them ever further West towards the magic glitter of the gold which was to be found in the rich black soil of California.

Mark stared at them as he stood by the bar. He was of them and yet apart from them. He watched them as they drank and laughed and wagered their hard-earned money. Some were prospectors drifting into town to get a new grub stake before venturing out into the Indian-infested wilds in their search for precious metals. Some were scouts, men who like himself, wore buckskin and watched with enigmatic eyes. A few were professional gamblers, smooth-faced, well-dressed, smiling without feeling as they dealt the cards, apparently unarmed, but with concealed Derringers up their arms or in hidden holsters. The majority were the restless, noisy hustlers from the wagon trains.

Young men mostly, though there were a plentiful scattering of grey-beards. Sober men usually, decent, hard-working men who had their eyes to the West and who were ready to undergo any hardship to get there. Now, on this the final stopping place which could be even remotely called civilised, they were having a final spree. Mark watched them, feeling the superiority of his experience and yet almost envying them their purpose in life.

He felt restless. Mrs Murphy had upset him more than she knew by her words, and he felt again the nagging doubt that he was wasting his time when he should be hard at work to rebuild what the war had destroyed. Irritably he moved towards a poker game and stood at the edge of the crowd to watch the interplay of bets across the green baize.

'Want in, mister?' The dealer smiled at him and gestured towards a vacant chair. Mark nodded, sat down and piled a small heap of gold coins before him.

'Ante ten dollars,' said the dealer. 'Jackpot, jacks to open.' He flipped round the cards with a professional skill. 'Openers?'

'I'll bet ten.' A young man to Mark's right shoved forward some money. Mark stared at his cards, saw a pair of tens, and added his ten dollars to the pot. The next man dropped out. Then next, a miner in a scarlet checked shirt, stayed. The dealer nodded.

'Discards.'

Mark dropped three cards and picked up another ten and a pair of fives. A full house, a good hand. The youth to his right drew two cards, the miner one, the dealer gave himself three.

'Bets?'

'Ten,' said the young man.

'Raise you ten,' said Mark.

'I pass,' said the miner. The dealer stayed, and it was up to the young man again.

'Raise twenty.'

'And twenty,' said Mark calmly, and pushed forward the extra dollars. The dealer glanced at him, peeped at his cards, shrugged, and tossed them on to the table.

'I pass.'

'Meet you and raise you twenty more.' The young man was deliberately casual, and Mark took time out to think. His opponent had drawn two cards. He had also opened so that meant he had either a pair or three of a kind. The betting was that he'd three so he could now have a full house or four of a kind. He could also be bluffing. Mark pushed forward some money.

'I'll raise you fifty.'

'And fifty more.'

'And fifty again.'

'I'll see you.' The youth glared at Mark. 'What've you got?'

'Full house. Tens high.'

'Good enough.' A muscle twitched high on the young man's cheek and he called for whisky. The dealer smiled as Mark gathered in the heap of coins.

'Heading for the goldfields?'

'Maybe.' Mark watched as the deal came round to the young man. For a while he played without any real interest in the game, betting, raising, winning and losing so that he stayed about even. The young man, however, was losing, and losing badly. The deal came round to the professional again, and Mark admired the deft way his slim fingers handled the cards.

'Openers?'

'I pass,' said the young man.

'Open for ten,' said Mark. No one raised and he drew another full house. 'Bet twenty.'

This time all but he, the gambler and the young man dropped out. The gambler raised, the young man raised again, and Mark shrugged as he pushed forward a hundred dollars.

'Raise you fifty.'

'And fifty more,' smiled the dealer.

'Hell,' swore the young man. 'I can't keep on losing, no luck can be that bad.' He fumbled in his pockets. 'Raise you a hundred.'

Mark dropped out. He wasn't winning and he wasn't losing, and he just didn't seem to get any excitement out of the game. The dealer fingered a pile of gold before him.

'Your hundred and I'll raise as much again.'

'I — ' Sweat beaded the young man's face. 'I don't know if I've got that much.'

'Then I win the pot,' smiled the gambler. 'You know the rules, put up or shut up. Well?'

'I'll see you.' Desperately the young man fumbled through his pockets. He found some coins, a few more, then produced a small leather bag tied with a thong. 'I've a little dust here. It's all I've got. Here.' He tossed it towards the centre of the table.

The gambler picked it up, loosened the thong and spilled out some of the grains. He peered at them, weighed the bag in his hand, and nodded.

'Okay. I've a set of aces. You?'

'Kings. Four of them.' The young man stared at the four aces the gambler laid face upwards on the table.

'Then you lose.' Calmly the gambler began to sweep the coins and gold towards him. 'You staying in?'

'You cheated!' The accusation came at the same time the young man went for his gun. Mark, watching him, thrust him to one side so that he fell off the rickety chair. Mark followed him, grunting as a fist slammed towards his jaw, then he was back on his feet, the young man's gun in his hand.

'Hold it!'

'He cheated,' snapped the young man. 'He had those aces up his sleeve, and I — '

'You lost,' said Mark flatly. 'There was no cheating and, even if there were, a gun is not the thing to settle it with. Better get back to your Pa, Youngster, before you get hurt.'

'Big talk,' sneered the youngster. 'Give me my gun and we'll see who talks the loudest.'

'Is anyone with this fool?' Mark stared around at the crowd. 'You?' He handed the gun to a bearded oldster. 'Take him out and cool him down. Let him come back in here and he'll get himself shot.'

He watched as the older man ushered the youngster out into the night.

'Thanks, stranger.' The gambler had left the table and now he nodded towards the bar. 'I'll take it kindly if you'd let me buy you a drink.'

'Why? What did I do?'

'Nothing, except maybe save my life.'

'The boy's life, you mean.' Mark looked at the neatly-dressed man at his side. 'You look like a man who can use a Derringer.'

'Maybe, but he had friends, and a professional gambler is never popular, especially when he's winning.' He held out his hand. 'May is my name. Friends call me Dancer. For reasons I would prefer not to enter into now. And yours?'

'Mark Young.'

'Captain Mark Young?' May smiled. 'I thought that I recognised you. We met once on the river boat at Natchez, during the early part of the war it was, before I got me a set of grey and went to fight the Yankees.' His smile became broader. 'Now you can't refuse to drink with me.'

Over the drinks he became more communicative.

'I'm glad the war's over,' he said frankly. 'Even though the South lost and is paying dearly for it. Civil War is the worse thing imaginable. Any war is bad, but a war which sets brother against brother is something straight from hell.' He sipped at his raw whisky. 'May I ask how fortune has treated you, sir?'

'I'm alive,' said Mark shortly. 'After the war there was nothing for me to go back to, so I turned trapper and trader. Then I became a scout, was attached to Fort Deacon for a while until the Indians quietened down. Now I'm just loafing around.'

'It's no time to be loafing,' said May seriously. 'Things are moving. All over the South people are packing up and heading West. From the shambles of war they are building a new country. What with the gold they've found in California, and now that the Indians have been put in their place, we can really stretch out.' He looked down at his glass. Seems a pity for a man to be wasting his time.'

Mark sighed. Here it was again, and this time from a comparative stranger. Mrs Murphy had been bad enough, but to hear the same talk from a gambler was even worse. Something of his impatience must have shown itself on his face, for May changed the subject.

'Tell me, Mark. You know the country. Any chance for a man like me to earn a living?'

'In California?'

'There, or anywhere.'

'Where there's gold there are saloons,' said Mark tersely. 'Where there are saloons you'll find gamblers. That answer enough for you?'

'I guess so.' Dancer stared around at the crowd. 'I've had my time here, anyway. Little money, and what there is seems to be snapped up by the people outfitting the wagon trains.' He tensed as he stared towards the wing doors. 'You expecting friends, Mark?'

'Not that I know of.'

'There's a couple of men seem to be interested in you. I've spotted them looking at you a couple of times and they've just looked in again.' May turned towards the mirror. 'Watch the doors, they'll be looking in again soon.'

Mark waited until the doors swung and a man's face stared towards him.

'That one?'

'Yes. I've seen them before, a couple of no-goods who work for the trading ring. Would they be interested in you for some reason?'

'They might.'

'Advice is cheap,' said May quietly. 'But Freeguard is wide open for all sorts of nastiness. One man, no matter how good, can't stop a dozen others from shooting him in the back.' He looked at Mark. 'Or two men, for that matter.'

'One man,' corrected Mark. He stared sombrely at the mirror. 'This trouble is my own.'

'Have you a horse?'

'Yes. A grey stallion. It's in the livery stable.'

'I'll get it,' said May. 'I'll take it round to the back. Any other stuff?'

'My roll is in the hotel.'

'I'll get that too. Which room?'

34

'I don't need a nurse,' said Mark coldly. 'I can collect my own stuff if and when I choose to move.'

'Suit yourself,' said the gambler, and moved towards a faro bank. Mark shrugged and concentrated on the two men watching him.

He saw them several times, dirty, ugly, unshaven men. Even among the rough crowd they seemed to stand out, for their dirt wasn't the honest marks of toil, but rather the slime which is to be found in the gutters. Killers, both of them, and both after Mark.

It was late when he left the saloon. He left through the back way, emerging into an alley ankle-deep with filth and redolent of rotting garbage. He trod carefully through the muck until he came to the boardwalk leading to his hotel. Inside the frame building he collected his roll, paid his bill and moved silently through the darkness towards the livery stable where he had lodged his horse. A shadow loomed before him, and he had almost knifed the man before he recognised the gambler.

'Your horse is tethered at the back with mine,' whispered May. He chuckled. 'They were so busy watching you they didn't notice me lead them out.'

'Thanks, but I told you that I didn't need a nurse.'

'You haven't got one,' said May softly. 'I've my own reasons for getting out of town and I figure that I'll live a lot longer if I'm with a man who knows the country.' His eyes gleamed in the starlight. 'That is, Captain, if you have no objection to company.'

Mark nodded, his eyes searching the star-lit dimness for signs of the men who were obviously out to get him. Something clicked across the street and to his right, a small sound as of a spur or a trigger being thumbed back to full cock. He crouched and the sound of the gambler's breathing was harsh in his ear.

'Two of them and more scattered down the street. What did you do,

Mark? Rob a bank?'

'Get on your horse,' breathed the tall man grimly. 'If you've got a gun get ready to use it. Those fellows mean business and it looks as if we've got to shoot our way out.'

The small sound echoed across the street again and, straining his eyes, Mark could see a shadow move slightly against the edge of a building. The movement had caused the man's spur to betray his position. Mark thinned his lips as he looked for the second man.

He found him, a hundred yards down the street, shielded behind a rain barrel as he watched the front of the livery stable. The fool was smoking, the poorly-shielded tip of his cigarette marking his position as though signalled in red lanterns. A horse whinnied from the rear of the stable and the man sprang upright, his cigarette falling into the muck and his hand clawing at his holster as he ran forward.

Mark shot him down with cold, calculated fury, thumbing back the hammer of his Colt and sending lead roaring down the street to smash the man's gun hand and send him yelling for help. He fired again, then again, as lead spat towards him; then he had ducked and run to the horse, was in the saddle and spurring his mount in a wild rush down the street and towards open country.

Dancer chuckled as he swung along beside him.

'Got him sweet as a whistle, Mark. Did they teach you to shoot like that in the cavalry?'

'Save your breath,' snapped the tall man. He was still burning with the fury he felt at having had to leave the town. To have remained would have meant sure death from a shot from some dark alley or a knife in the back, but he hated having to leave because he had killed a man in fair fight. Freeguard was, as Mrs Murphy had said, a place which could do with some law and order. Gun law was all right while it was one man against another, but it fell down when

38

gangs administered it and protected their own with certain death for any who harmed them.

They had reached the outskirts of town, and the prairie opened out before them, when from a huddle of wagons gunfire blazed towards them. The trading ring of which Fred had been the head and leader was determined to get the man who had shown them up and done them so much harm.

'Duck.' Mark crouched in the saddle, a trick he had used often when charging towards the enemy during the war. He used the body of the horse to shield him, firing from beside its neck, and the horse, well trained as it was, stretched its legs as it put distance between the men hidden in the wagons and itself.

For a moment the firing continued, a scatter of shots fired more from bravado than from any real hope of hitting either of the men. The night, the darkness and the dimly-seen shapes made accurate shooting impossible and the flurry of lead sent after Mark and

Dancer was dictated by hate more than judgment.

'We're in the clear.' Mark pulled at the reins and slowed from a gallop into a walk. 'They won't follow us and even if they do we can see them before they see us.' He peered into the darkness towards his companion. 'Dancer! You hurt?'

'Some.' The gambler winced as he slowed his horse. 'Shoulder, I think. I —'

He toppled, falling as a tree would fall, stiff and helpless as he swayed from the saddle. Mark caught him, replaced him in his seat, and led the horses to the side of the road. A brief examination told him that the gambler was lucky to still be alive.

The bullet had struck him in the back, low on the left side, and it must have lodged somewhere near the heart. The bleeding alone showed that immediate attention was essential if there was to be any hope, and Mark stared back towards the town as he supported the unconscious figure of the gambler.

To return meant riding straight into the men who had tried to kill him. To continue meant that the gambler would die. There was only one thing he could do.

Getting his direction from the stars he rode slowly and carefully towards the north edge of the town. It took almost an hour before he saw the camp fires of the wagon train and, by the time the guards hailed him, his own buckskins were wet with the gambler's blood. Quickly he identified himself and asked to speak to either Blake or Henderson. Blake answered the sentry's call and Mark told him what had happened.

'We'll take him in, sure,' said the bearded wagon boss, 'but as for doctoring him, hell, we ain't got no doctor with us.'

'Have you got a wagon I can use? Some lights? A medical kit?' While he was talking Mark had dismounted and seen to it that the gambler was as

41

comfortable as he could be made. Blake nodded.

'We can fix you up. You aim to operate on him yourself?'

'You know anyone else who can do it?'

'No.'

'Then get me the lights, some hot water, a bottle of whisky and your medical kit. And hurry.'

The wagon used for the operation had hastily been cleared of its load. The lights were lanterns, smoking and odorous and casting a poor light. His nurse was one of the women who had often helped at other primitive operations. Quickly Mark stripped off his buckskins, washed his hands and arms with whisky and selected a set of probes. Turning the unconscious gambler on to his face he nodded to the men standing by.

'Right. Cut his clothes off and hold him tight.' He waited until they had set themselves. 'Tight now; if he jumps around it'll mean curtains.'

Carefully he probed the wound, trying not to hurry at the sight of the welling blood and yet knowing that unless he hurried he would be wasting his time. He grunted as the slender probes touched the bullet, then carefully he extracted the hunk of lead.

'Got it! Water!'

He used it to cleanse the wound, held out his hand for the whisky bottle and poured the raw spirit into the open wound. May groaned, heaved, then relaxed as the men holding him tightened their grip.

'Now we'll plug it,' said Mark harshly. 'Then we'll bandage him and let him lie. Either he'll be lucky and escape infection and recover, or he'll be unlucky and die.' He wiped his hands and reached for the whisky bottle. 'He was lucky to be unconscious to begin with; saved me having to knock him out.' He tilted the bottle, swallowed and passed it to one of the men.

'Take care of this for me, will you?' He smiled at the woman. 'Can I leave him in your care, ma'am?'

'I'll watch for him,' she said. 'I'll watch him real good.'

'Thank you.' Mark stretched, frowned at the blood on his trousers and buckskins and, picking up his weapon belt, jumped from the back of the wagon.

Blake was waiting for him beside the camp fire. 'Coffee?' He held out a tin mug full of the scalding brew and Mark accepted. Tiredly he sat down, warming himself at the blaze, feeling the reaction from hard action and near death leave him as he relaxed.

'Thanks.'

'How's your friend?'

'He'll make out — one way or the other.'

Blake fidgeted. 'Look Mark, I don't want to rush you, but as I told you, we pull out at dawn.' He hesitated. 'I — '

'You don't want to carry a sick man, is that it?'

'That's it.'

'He's bad,' said Mark tiredly. 'He shouldn't be moved at all, but he's got nowhere else to go. Even riding a wagon would be better for him than going back to Freeguard. They know he helped me and they'd kill him on sight.'

'You want for us to take him with us?' Blake looked dubious. 'It's a hard road, Mark, you said so yourself, and tough one. Maybe he'll die on the way.'

'So what if he does? Death now, death later, don't it all add up to the same in the end?' Mark stared at the wagon boss. 'You made me a proposition a while back. You got a scout yet?'

'No.'

'You've got one now. I'll lead you to California; if you'll take the gambler to Fort Deacon. It's not too hard a trip and we can leave him there. Is it a deal?'

Blake nodded. 'It's a deal.'

Mark felt almost too tired to shake hands on it.

3

Dawn came and with it the camp bustled into a hive of activity. Mark rose, washed himself in a bucket, and gulped gratefully at the hot coffee before tucking into the bacon and beans served to all from the great communal cooking pot suspended over the fire. Breakfast over, the entire camp swung into the business of breaking up and getting on the trail.

Before the sun was an hour in the sky the wagons had been loaded, the oxen harnessed and the train moving with creaking wheels and swaying canopies towards the West.

Riding his horse easily at the head of the train Mark surveyed it with experienced eyes. It was the usual train, one of hundreds that had started out full of hope and ambition towards the golden promise of free land, plentiful game and, more recently, the glitter of gold from the newly discovered fields in California. Many such trains had arrived safely. Many others had vanished in the limitless expanses of the Middle West, others had crawled into the safety of the scattered forts, their oxen starving, their men-folk killed, their wagons burned and looted by rampaging Indians or had succumbed to the rigours of desert and mountain.

Looking at this train Mark felt his first doubts,

The wagons were regular Connestogas, high built, solid, big wheeled and each with the high canopy which sheltered the interior and made of the wagons both conveyances and homes for the families who owned them. Each wagon was pulled by six or eight oxen, most had cows tied to their rears, some had crates of chickens or young pigs loaded together with farming tools, sacks of seed and grain and the few items of household furniture with which to start a new life.

Around the train, riding to either side, to the rear and van, young men on horseback trotted, altering their pace so as to keep moving alongside the wagons and calling out to the elderly men with their wives who rode on the driving seats, or winking at the young girls who peeped from the open rears. Young children were there too, boys and moppets laughing and talking as they jolted over the rolling prairie. It was, in effect, as if an entire community was on the move, self-sufficient, self-sustaining, ready to outspan and settle down at a favourable spot, there to break dirt and start farms, to rear houses and found schools, to give birth to new townships where only the buffalo had hitherto been known.

Yet Mark, as he stared at the creaking wagons, didn't like what he saw.

Little things mostly, but little things which could cause trouble later on. He rode up to the lead wagon and, with a lithe motion, slipped from his saddle to the front of the wagon. Blake smiled at him and handed the reins to his wife.

'Hi, Mark. Like what you see?'

'No.'

A shadow touched the old man's eyes. He glanced at his wife, a tough farmer's wife, her face sun tanned in the shelter of her poke bonnet, and jerked his head towards the interior of the wagon.

Mark nodded to the woman and followed him inside.

A girl sat sewing on a box. A young girl, fresh with the bloom of her early spring, neat and clean in her voluminous skirts and poke bonnet. She stared at Mark with even, blue eyes, and he waited patiently for Blake to introduce them.

'Mark, this is Shelia, my daughter. Shelia, Mark Young who is our guide.' He chuckled. 'Guess you young folk didn't get much chance to see each other last night.'

'I arrived late,' said Mark, and doffed his hat. Blake looked at Shelia.

'Sit up front with your mother, girl.

The air will do you good.' He waited until she had squeezed past them then looked at Mark. 'Well?'

'A fine girl you have there, Mr Blake. Engaged?'

'She says not, though young Walt Shaw reckons that he owns her.'

'He's a lucky man.'

'Maybe. You ain't seen Walt yet.' Blake stared at Mark. 'Well? We didn't come in here to talk about Shelia.'

'That's right.' Mark hesitated, knowing how touchy some wagon bosses were and knowing too that he was only the scout and that it was really none of his business. He looked at Blake. 'You asked me if I liked what I saw and I said no. You want me to tell you why?'

'That's the idea.'

'I'll give it to you straight. Someone's got to bear down on these people or none of them will ever make it. Listen to those wheels! No wheels should sound like that just after leaving a set-down stage. Why weren't they greased? And another thing. Five of the water barrels are leaking, three of the wagons have no spare tyres for their wheels, two of them are pulled by oxen which will die within the first week unless they are given a rest. I'll put it this way, Blake. You may be responsible, as wagon boss you are, but this is no way to set out for the West.'

Blake flushed, but didn't immediately answer. Instead he moved to the back of the wagon and called out to a rider passing by.

'Jeff! Send Walt up here, will you! Urgent!'

'Is Walt the boss?' said Mark dryly. Blake nodded.

'Yes. We had a meeting after I saw you and they elected him to lead them.' Blake shrugged. 'They still let me ride lead wagon, but I guess they thought that they owed me that much. Anyway, with Walt feeling the way he does about Shelia, they thought that it didn't matter. All in the family as you might say.'

'Is it?'

'Walt's a nice young lad,' said Blake slowly. 'A bit wild maybe, but who ain't when young? The trouble is that he's got gold-fever, and you know what that means.'

Mark nodded then looked up as a young man swung himself through the open back of the wagon.

Recognition was immediate and mutual. Walt Shaw, the new wagon boss, was the same man who had lost at poker and had tried to draw a gun.

'You!' He lurched towards Mark, who sat, not moving, on the edge of a box. Blake looked from one to the other in surprise.

'You know each other?'

'We met,' said Mark briefly. He wasn't going to enter into details and, from his expression, neither was Walt. 'Blake tells me that you're the new wagon boss?'

'Blake don't lie. What of it?'

'Nothing,' said Mark quietly. 'Except that I know the country ahead and you don't. The way I see it is that unless you take time out to fix the wagons you just ain't all going to make it.' Deliberately he thickened his voice and spoke the speech which a normal scout would use. He nodded towards Blake. 'I've told Blake what's wrong and maybe you'd like for me to tell you. The wagons need to be taken care of, the water barrels fixed and the oxen evened out. A day should do it.'

'A day.' Walt looked anxious. 'Hell, we've lost enough time already. The men are eager to get to the fields while there's still a chance of grabbing a decent stake. A day might make all the difference.'

Mark sighed. He had met gold-fever before, the insane urge after the yellow metal which made men lose their sense of proportion and forget everything but the glitter at the rainbow's end.

'If you're smart,' he said evenly, 'you'll lose a day now instead of maybe a couple of weeks later. The train should never have left Freeguard in the state it's in. Even you should have known better than that.'

'We've come a long way,' said Blake hastily. 'We didn't have much time.'

'You'll have less if a couple of the wagons break down,' reminded Mark. He rose. 'Well, it's none of my worry. I'll take a look over the hill while you talk about it.'

He climbed to the front of the wagon and whistled to his horse. Nodding to the two women he mounted and rode a few miles ahead of the wagon train. This close to Freeguard there was little danger, but he knew from long experience that the unexpected was always to be reckoned with. He swung in a wide circle, scouting the prairie for several miles, and didn't return to the train until it was getting towards the end of the day. He was tired from long hours in the saddle, but tired as he was he watched as the line of wagons manoeuvred into position for the night.

Then he sent his horse loping towards them.

The wagons had stopped in an

irregular line, and already the thin smoke of cooking fires was rising towards the sky as the women prepared the evening meal. The oxen, relieved of their yokes, lowed as they muzzled their feed and the horses cropped at the scant grass, watched over by a couple of boys barely in their teens.

Mark accepted a mug of coffee, sniffed at the appetising smell coming from the big cooking pot, and nodded to Henderson.

'Glad to see you with us, Mark,' the old man said. 'Blake told me what happened and, though I'm sorry to hear about your friend, I'd rather it happen this way than not at all.'

'Thank you.' Mark nodded to Mrs Henderson and ruffled the hair of a red-headed boy of about twelve. 'Your son, Mr Henderson?'

'Yes.' Henderson smiled proudly at the boy. 'This is Skip, Mark. Skip, meet Mark Young, one of the best scouts and Indian fighters alive.'

'Gee!' Hero-worship shone in the

boy's eyes. 'Indian fighter, huh? Is it true that the Apaches string you up and skin you alive if they catch you?'

'Not exactly,' said Mark, smiling at the eagerness in the boy's voice. 'But it's best not to be caught by them if you can help it.'

'Have you ever been caught by them, Mark? Have you shot many? Is it true that — '

'Save it for later, Skip,' said Mark. 'I've been riding all day and I'm about all in. You got a horse?'

'Sure. A gun too. Pop gave me a real Winchester for my birthday last year and I can use it.'

'Fine. Tell you what, you ride out with me tomorrow and I'll tell you about the Indians. That's if your folks have no objection.'

'Gee!' Skip swallowed and looked at his father. Henderson smiled at him and nodded.

'He can go with you, Mark. Have you eaten?'

'Not yet.'

'Sit in with us. Mrs Henderson's a better cook than most, though I say so myself, and you'll eat better with us than at the cooking-pot.' He smiled towards his wife. 'Ain't that so, Martha?'

'Sarah's a good cook too, Bill,' she smiled. 'Sarah's Blake's wife and she's in charge of the big pot,' she explained. 'Shelia helps her. You seen Shelia yet?'

'This morning.'

'Nice girl, Shelia,' said the woman. 'Time somebody up and married her. She'll make some lucky man a good wife.'

'Walt Shaw?'

'He figures so, but if you ask me Shelia's got other ideas.' She gestured towards Mark with a wooden spoon. 'Set down and fill up. Riding makes a man hungry.'

Mark grinned and sat beside the fire. While waiting for Martha to fill a plate with an appetising mess of stew he looked over the camp. Before each wagon a small fire had been lit for purposes of cooking the evening meal. Each family cooked for themselves, and a larger fire, one that would be fed all night, served to cook for the outriders, the young men serving as guards, the scouts and others attached to the wagon train. A few single men ate there too, not bothering to cook for themselves, but adding supplies to the communal pot.

It was the usual system for wagon trains. A compromise between communal living and the retention of family and private groups. Each wagon carried its own supplies and, should they feel like it, any wagon was free to leave the train at any time. Others too could join, subject only to the discipline of the wagon boss, whose word was law. He had a responsible job. It was he who decided when and where camps should be made, the route taken and the employment of scouts and guides. A good boss could make a hard journey easier, a bad one could ruin a train and leave it to moulder on the desert.

Mark didn't think that Walt would make a good boss.

The stew finished, he relaxed, lighting a thin cigar and listening to the thrum of a guitar someone was playing. Spirits were high now and everyone eager to be on the move. He wondered just how long that enthusiasm would last.

Henderson, his bearded face dim in the firelight, looked at Mark, jerked his head to one side and, rising, led the way from the camp. Mark followed him, his booted feet whispering on the sparse grass of the sunbaked prairie.

'Carl tells me that you ain't happy about the condition of the wagons,' snapped Henderson abruptly. 'He tells me that you told Walt and Walt didn't like it.'

'That's right.'

'You still feel the same way?'

'More so.'

'How's that?'

'The way you've set up camp tonight. If there was an Indian raid you wouldn't stand a chance.'

'Indian raid! Hell, there ain't no Indians this close, are there?'

'No, but there will be later on.' Mark dragged at his cigar, the glowing tip outlining the harsh lines of his face. 'Listen, Henderson, I'm only the guide and scout, not the boss. But if you want this train to get through to California someone had better start taking some advice. First thing is to make a ring camp at night. Wagons on the outside, horses and oxen on the inside, and regular guards posted to keep watch. Setting up camp that way takes time unless you've practised. And you'd better start practising soon. You may have to make a ring camp at any time, and all the warning you'll get will be a couple of shots or one of the scouts coming towards you with an Indian at his heels. I've already told Walt about the rest of what's wrong.'

'Walt's young and hot-headed, but he ain't dumb,' said Henderson. 'He's going to make an overhaul at Fort

Deacon. How long do you reckon we'll be getting there?'

'At the rate we're going say a couple of weeks. Better get Walt to spread out the oxen a bit. Some of the beasts look as though they won't make it.'

'I'll see to it,' promised Henderson. 'Anything else?'

'I'll think of something.' Mark stared towards the wagons. 'I'd better look in at Dancer. See you.'

He moved into the fireglow, tall, spare, and somehow giving the impression of ruthless efficiency. Men nodded at him as he passed; already he was known to all the train, and he doffed his hat as a woman came towards him.

'How's the patient, ma'am?'

'Awake.' She rubbed toil-worn hands against her apron. 'He had a rough trip, Mark, and I think he's getting a fever.'

'I'll look in at him,' said Mark. 'Anyone with him?'

'My daughter, Mary. She's been tending him during the journey.'

'He's trouble,' said Mark. He looked

at the woman. 'How does your man feel about it?'

'My man's dead,' she said. 'A rattlesnake got him four days from home. Me and Mary have been trying to make it without him. It hasn't been easy.'

He nodded, knowing just what she meant. Driving the wagon, harnessing the oxen, collecting fuel for the fire and wrestling with the heavy supplies was too much work for any woman. She would have been helped of course, women were held in too high regard for any man to stand by and refuse his assistance, but everyone had too much work to do and, in the nature of things, life would have been far from easy for the widow and her daughter.

'You've got a nice wagon there. Home built?'

'Marvin built it from the best wood he could get,' she said proudly. 'His tools are inside, he was a carpenter, and I've kept them with me just in case.' She shrugged with the surface hardness of the pioneer. 'No sense in grieving over the dead, Mark. Better take a look at your friend while he's still awake.'

Mark nodded and sprang up into the wagon.

Dancer turned his head as Mark came towards him and tried to smile. The gambler looked ghastly. His sallow features were stained with sweat and his eyes were sunken back into his head. He winced as he moved, and as Mark touched his pulse he began to throw off the blankets covering him.

Mary, the girl at his side, gently but firmly put them back. She looked at Mark.

'Well?'

'Too early to tell yet,' he said with brutal abruptness. He stared down at the gambler. 'It's up to you, Dancer. If you want to live hard enough you will. If you start feeling sorry for yourself and give up the fight, then you'll be crow-meat. Anything you want?'

'A bottle of whisky would help,' said the gambler. 'That or a gun. This damn wagon ain't what you'd call a feather bed, you know.'

'You're lucky to be alive at all,' snapped Mark. He grinned down at the pale face of the gambler. 'Don't lie there longer than you have to, fellow. There's work to do and only a couple of women to do it. Eat well, don't drink too much and don't drink whisky at all. Try and sleep as long as you can.' He rested his hand on Dancer's shoulder. 'You'll make it, fellow. The crows can starve if they're depending on you. Don't let me down.'

He grinned again and jumped from the tail of the wagon. He waited, and within a few seconds Mary Marvin joined him. She looked pale and annoyed and stared at Mark with furious eyes.

'A fine way to treat your friend,' she stormed. 'I suppose you think it big to talk like that when he's lying sick and ill?'

'Take it easy.' Taking her arm he steered her away from the wagon and towards the central fire. 'Listen. I've treated wounds before and I know what to do. Dancer has got to heal himself, no one can do it for him. Once he begins to believe that everyone feels sorry for him he will lose that much drive to recover. I'm sorry, Mary, but I know what I am doing. A man always fights better when he's in a temper.'

'He's sick, Mark. How sick?'

'Bad,' he admitted. 'He should be in hospital or in bed at least. The jolting of the wagon isn't doing him a bit of good, but as long as he fights he's got a chance. Are you nursing him?'

'Yes.'

'Feed him plenty of broth. Keep him covered, especially at night. I don't want him to catch pneumonia. I'll drop in towards dawn and take over for a spell.' He smiled at her small, round, almost childish face lost beneath her poke bonnet. 'How old are you, Mary?'

'Eighteen. Why?'

'Nothing, but just remember that Dancer is a hunk of perforated meat and that you're his nurse. Get what I mean?'

She flushed and turned abruptly away. Mark grinned after her, then as he began a slow way around the camp lost his grin.

Around him the camp was settling to sleep. Hard work and a dawn to sunset drive left little energy for amusements at night and, as soon as everyone had eaten, the women chased the children to bed, the youngsters swapped yarns, while the older men smoked and, while it was still early, all retired to their blankets save for the few men posted as guards.

Mark yawned, found his blankets and, rolling them around himself, lay smoking and staring up at the sky. About his head the stars glittered across the bowl of heaven as bright and as hard as if they were a double handful of diamonds tossed there by some careless jeweller. He stared at them for a long time, remembering other nights when he had stared at a similar sky, then crushing out his cigar he turned on his side and went to sleep.

4

The first arguments started the next day. Mark heard the sound of raised voices and, gulping his morning coffee, went across to see what all the noise was about. He found young Walt, his face red, his eyes dangerous, staring at a white-faced man wearing a check shirt, grease-stained pants and the regular high boots.

'Look,' said Walt lightly. 'You've got more oxen than you need. Why not loan a couple of them to Mrs Marvin? Her team's about all in.'

'Is that my fault?' The sullen-faced man kicked at the ground. 'I aim to get to California and I need them oxen to get there. If Mrs Marvin can't make it with the team she's got then maybe she'd better turn back to Freeguard.'

'That ain't no way to talk, Sanson,' snapped Walt. 'As the boss around here

I'm telling you to — '

'Hold it.' Mark thrust himself forward. 'Look, Sanson, put it this way. Will you hire a couple of your beasts to the widow while hers rest up?'

'Well — ' The man hesitated. 'I don't aim to be hard, but you know how it is. Anything can happen, one of my team break a leg or something like that. I don't aim to be stranded because I gave away my spare oxen.'

'You won't be,' promised Mark. 'Look, loan her a couple and you can have the use of Dancer's horse. How's that?'

Sanson hesitated some more, but Mark could see that he was wavering. He nodded.

'Okay. You lend me the horse and I'll lend her a couple of oxen. If I want 'em back at any time I get them. She feeds them and I feed the horse. That suit you?'

'Fine.' Mark pulled at Walt's sleeve and drew him out of earshot.

'Listen, Walt, you ever been wagon boss before?'

'What's it to you?'

'Maybe nothing, maybe a lot. Listen, Walt, let's forget what happened in the saloon. We've got something more important to worry about now. Have you?'

'No.'

'I thought not. Look, Walt, being wagon boss doesn't make you owner of all the goods and gear. Sanson has a right to keep his own beasts and you've no right to do more than ask him to lend them out. Trade, yes, ask, yes, order, no.'

'He can't use them,' protested Walt. 'It wouldn't hurt him to have lent them.'

'That isn't the point. Would you lend out your horse just for the asking? Of course you wouldn't. Sanson is the same and so is every other man. They're decent enough, but they want to get to the West and they can't be expected to wet-nurse everyone with a bad wagon or a broken-down team.' Mark grinned at the young man. 'Get what I mean?'

'I think so.' Walt still looked offended. 'I hear that you don't like the way I'm running things.'

'I didn't say that. I said that maybe it would be a good idea to take some advice. Look, Walt, I've been over this country a dozen times. I've seen what happens to wagon trains with careless bosses. You may see it too. There are women and children in those wagons, and the Indians don't care who they kill when they're on the warpath. The desert don't care either. Take my advice and at Fort Deacon take some time out to get ready for the desert crossing. It's a hard pull and a long one and will take all you've got.'

'Maybe you should be the boss,' said Walt bitterly. 'Is that what you want?'

'No. I'm hired to act as scout and guide. I'll do my job, but I expect others to do theirs. I'll tell you this, Walt, unless things alter by the time we reach Fort Deacon you can get yourself another scout. I don't aim to lose my scalp and I don't want to see others lose theirs. Think it over.'

He swung away and returned to his interrupted breakfast.

He was mopping up the last of the beans and bacon when Skip yelled to him from the Henderson wagon.

'Hey, Mark! Ready?'

Mark looked up at the boy and grinned in welcome. Skip, neatly dressed in Levis and high boots, came swaggering towards him, one thumb tucked into his belt.

'Hello, soldier. Eager to get moving?'

'Sure am, Mark. Will we see any Indians?'

'I hope not. Eaten yet?'

'I'm not hungry.'

'If you don't eat then you don't ride with me,' said Mark sternly. 'Riding takes it out of a man and I don't aim to have to carry you back in. Fill up now while I see to my horse.'

He left Skip forcing himself to eat and nodded to Henderson.

'I'll take care of him, Mr Henderson. Sure you can spare him?'

72

'I'm sure.' The old man grunted as he tightened a lashing. 'It's time he found his own feet, Mark, and I take it kindly that you're willing to be bothered with him. I've packed his canteen and grub roll. What time do you figure on getting back?'

'Maybe mid-day, or maybe not until evening. I want to take a wide swing: I'll sleep easier knowing that no one's around to disturb it.'

He touched his hat to Mrs Henderson, looked in at Dancer, then found his own horse. He checked his saddle, his Winchester and the blanket roll tied back of the saddle. By the time he had finished, Skip had mounted and was riding towards him.

'Come on, Mark. They'll be moving soon and we haven't even started.'

'First lesson,' said Mark. 'You don't leave the train without telling the boss where you're going. We do that first.'

Walt was busy harnessing his team when Mark approached him.

'I'm riding to the north and west,' he

said. 'Don't expect to find anything, but I'd like to make sure. Which way you heading?'

'Due west.'

'Right. Due west it is.' Mark nodded and, gathering his reins, rode off, Skip by his side. Behind them the shouts of men echoed over the prairie as the wagons jerked into motion. Mark paused, looking back at them, then joined Skip who was impatiently waiting for him.

For a while they rode in silence, each busy with his own thoughts, then Skip, impatient with the impatience of youth, broke the silence.

'You killed many men, Mark?'

'Some.'

'How many? Ten? Twenty?'

'I forget.' Mark spurred his horse and rode to the brow of a low hill. He rode over the skyline, then halted, his keen grey eyes surveying the country before him. To the north the dark ridges of wooded hills thrust above the prairie. He turned to see Skip still on the brow of the hill, his young face intent as he stared about him.

'Skip! Get down here. Fast!'

'Something wrong?' Skip jerked at his reins and pulled his horse to a stop beside him.

'Never stay on a skyline, Skip. You can be seen for miles that way. Always get below it so that it's behind you before you take a look around.

'Oh.' The boy's disappointment was plain. 'I thought that you'd seen Indians.'

'I don't want to see Indians,' said Mark curtly. 'Indian fighting isn't fun, Skip. Too many people get hurt that way. Never forget that it's a lot better to dodge a fight than to get in one. Trouble is the one thing that's easy to find. A wise man stays out of trouble.'

'Aw, Mark,' said Skip disgustedly. 'I thought that we'd get some action out here. Back in the train there's nothing to do but hold the reins or do the chores. I'm getting tired of that sort of thing.' Unconsciously his hand fell to the new Winchester sitting in the saddle scabbard. Mark saw the gesture and smiled.

'You're dying to try out that new rifle, aren't you?'

'Well, anything wrong in that?'

'Not when you shoot at a bottle or something like that. You might even hit a coyote or deer, but think twice before you get an Indian in your sight. In that case you shoot when you have to and then you shoot fast and often.' He held out his hand. 'Let me see that rifle.'

Skip lifted it from its leather and passed it over. Mark took it, operating the lever and studying the action. He caught the expelled bullet and thrust it back into the magazine. He hefted the weapon, lifted it to his shoulder and squinted down the barrel. He handed it back.

'Okay, Mark?'

'It's a good gun. One of the new ones that came out just too late to help us in the war. The trouble is that when a man's got a warehouse full of guns he wants to get rid of them. So the traders started exchanging them for furs and other stuff from the Indians. Now we've reached the point where a lot of the Indians are better armed than the cavalry. Those boys still use their carbines.'

'Springfields?'

'That's right. I did hear that there's going to be a new issue of Springfields soon. Bolt action jobs which should make them more equal in fire power to the Indians.'

'I don't get it, Mark,' said Skip, frowning. 'If the Indians are so better armed why is it that the cavalry can always beat them?'

'Not always, Skip. But the real reason is that the Indian doesn't fight like the white man. To him war is a sport, they go on a raid, burn a few wagons or maybe a settlement, and then go back to their camps and call the war off. We don't do that. We just keep on fighting all the time, so the Indians can't really ever win.' He stared sombrely over the sparse grasslands. 'There are other reasons, but that's one of them.'

'What are the others?' Skip was eager to hear more. 'Is it true that the Apaches torture their prisoners?'

'Sometimes.'

'Have you ever killed an Apache, Mark?'

'Yes.'

'Many of them?'

'A few.' Mark turned in his saddle. 'Don't make the mistake a lot of people make, Skip. The Indian is no savage. He has a different way of life from us, but that doesn't mean he isn't intelligent. They just don't think as we do, that's all. They don't unite for one thing, and an Apache chief has no real power. If an Indian doesn't want to fight there's nothing to make him. If he decides to go home and get ready for the winter, he does. Can you imagine what would happen if our own soldiers did that?'

'They'd be shot for desertion,' said Skip promptly.

'That's right. But no one Indian will

accept anything remotely like discipline from another, not even his own chief. You have to persuade an Indian, you can't order him, and that's why they don't, and can't fight as we do.'

'I see.' Skip rode in silence for a while. 'Mark.'

'Yes?'

'You were in the war, weren't you, Mark?'

'I was.'

'North or South?'

'South.'

'The losing side.' Skip shrugged. 'Well, someone had to lose.'

'Everyone loses in war, Skip. Don't let's talk about it now. Look, see that mound over there?'

'Yep.'

'Race you to the top.'

Immediately they both spurred their horses and went racing towards the distant mound. For a while they rode neck and neck, then, as Mark's skill and superior mount began to tell over the boy's lightness, he drew ahead. He was all of a hundred yards in the lead when he reached the brow of the mound. He topped it, rode over it and halted and dismounted by the time Skip joined him.

'What is it, Mark?'

'Look.' Mark pointed to a burnt patch before him. Tensely he felt the ashes, moved them away and probed at the dirt beneath. Picking up some of the ash he crumpled it between his fingers, sniffed at it, then threw it away. He stared thoughtfully about him as he wiped his fingers on his buckskins.

'Someone's had a camp fire here,' said Skip indifferently. 'Nothing to worry about.'

'Come here, Skip,' ordered Mark. 'Feel those ashes, smell them, taste them.' He waited until the boy had done as he was told. 'That's a buffalochip fire, Skip. The Indians collect the dried droppings from the buffalo herds and use them for fuel.'

'Indians!'

'Yes. This fire was lit last night and it

80

was an Indian fire.' Mark began to stalk around the patch of ash, his eyes narrowed as he studied the ground. 'A small party, I guess. Maybe ten or twelve warriors. They slept here and moved on well before dawn.'

'A war party?' Skip was excited. He ran to his horse and jerked out his rifle, his eyes eager as he looked for a painted target. Mark snatched the weapon from his hands and slammed it back into its scabbard.

'Don't go off half-cocked, Skip. It may not have been a war party at all. I'd guess that it wasn't. A war party wouldn't light a fire, but a hunting party would. In any case, they've gone by now.'

'Maybe they're watching us, Mark!' Skip stared at the wooded hills now close to them. 'Maybe they're getting all ready to charge us and string us up and carve us to pieces like they do all their prisoners.'

'You've been listening to too many tall stories,' snapped Mark disgustedly.

He sniffed at the air and stared about him. Slowly he mounted and waited for Skip to join him. Thoughtfully he began to ride back in the general direction of the wagon train.

'You going back, Mark?'

'Not yet. I want to scout around a little more first. We're beginning to leave the prairie now and I want to see what lies ahead. Use your eyes from now on, Skip, and no talking unless you have to.'

He smiled to himself as they rode along. He could guess at the images Skip's imagination had conjured up, fed by wild, camp-fire stories, and he probably believed that an Indian lurked behind every bush and hillock. Mark knew better, but he also knew more, and he was frowning as he rode along.

Indian parties were unusual this close to Freeguard. Between the town and Fort Deacon stretched the last of the prairie before it merged with the blistering hell of the desert. That had to be crossed and the foothills climbed before the train could begin the last leg of the journey to California. Most trains were attacked well past the fort by Indians, who struck from the rugged terrain and retreated back to the safety of their wooded hills far to the north.

It was a long journey and tedious. Dangerous for more reasons than one, but lately people had begun to consider the first stretch between Freeguard and Fort Deacon as just another wagon route. Safe, well-travelled, free from danger.

Mark hoped that it was going to stay that way.

He rode until the sun had climbed well above the horizon, and then he called a halt for a meal and a rest. Skip climbed stiffly from his saddle and was about to gather wood for a fire when Mark stopped him.

'We'll eat cold, Skip. No sense in lighting a fire until you're ready to settle down for the night.' He rummaged in his bag and produced a piece of bread and a chunk of jerked deer meat.

Slicing off a piece with his hunting knife he passed it to Skip, who began to chew at the tough meat without relish.

'Get used to it, Skip. A scout's life isn't always fighting Indians and roistering in saloons. To be a good scout and Indian fighter you've got to be as good as an Indian himself. That means you must be able to go for days without food, live on a handful of corn or a bit of dried meat, and sleep out in all weathers. You should be able to read signs, tell the weather from the way the clouds look, and live in a region where a goat would starve.' He tore off a piece of the jerked meat with his strong white teeth and pointed with his knife.

'Take you, for instance. Twelve years old and still wet behind the ears. An Indian boy at your age can run all day without stopping, can break a horse, shoot with bows and arrows, trap and skin beaver, fox, bear and deer, ride without a saddle and has probably been out on his first raid.'

'Yeah,' said Skip. 'But can he fix a

wagon wheel, harness oxen, handle a plough and mix his own powder? I can.'

'Good for you,' said Mark. 'But the point I'm making is this. To live in Indian country you've got to be constantly alert. It doesn't help you none to be able to fix a wagon wheel when a war party's after you and howling for your scalp.'

He grinned at the boy's discomfited expression and chewed on his dry meat. Skip was young and, like all young men, thought that he knew it all. But he was willing to learn and eager for experience. Mark only hoped that he wouldn't have to learn the hard way.

The meal finished, they remounted and struck down towards the south. Somewhere in that direction the wagon train was crawling on its route towards Fort Deacon, and Mark hoped that they had made good time. The wagons were slow, they moved at little more than a walking pace, but they never stopped from dawn till dusk, and even a slow train can travel a long distance in a day if it doesn't stop.

They were riding past a clump of thin trees when Mark reined and dropped from his saddle. Skip followed him, his Winchester in his hand, and this time Mark didn't take it from him.

Carefully he eased forward between the trees, the long-barrelled Colt in his hand, the hammer drawn back under his thumb. Skip, hardly daring to breathe, followed him, the rifle at the ready.

Mark halted and stared at something before him, then, his face grim, he looked at Skip.

'Stay here.'

'Why, Mark? What is it?'

'A man, wounded or dead. Cover me while I scout around.'

Skip nodded, the rifle slippery with the sweat from his palms, and Mark disappeared into the trees without a rustle to betray his presence. For a long time nothing seemed to happen, and then Mark called to him in a low voice.

'Right, Skip. Come out now and

bring the canteen.'

The man wasn't dead. Skip stared down at his contorted features while Mark moistened the pallid lips with water. The man was a prospector, old, wizened, and his eyes when he opened them were peculiarly opaque and mottled.

'Indians?' Mark wasted no time. The man tried to nod.

'Yeah. They caught me and my partner way back in the hills. We ran for it, thought we'd dodge them, then ran into another party.' He coughed, blood welling from his mouth and, as he tried to rise, Skip saw the broken shank of an arrow protruding from his back.

'Take it easy, old-timer,' said Mark gently. 'Where's your partner?'

'Dead. I saw him fall a way back, head split with a tomahawk. I made a run for it and they shot me. Fell off my horse and crawled in here.' Incredibly he tried to grin. 'Kept my scalp anyways. I — '

He sighed and relaxed. Mark stared

down at him, his cold eyes thoughtful, then, stooping, he closed the dead eyes.

'You were wrong,' said Skip sickly. 'That was a war party.'

'No.' Mark turned over the dead man, and with a sharp tug pulled out the broken arrow. 'See, no barbs. This is a hunting arrow not a war arrow. Not that it makes any difference now, he's dead just the same.' He turned towards his horse and Skip followed him.

'Ain't you going to bury him, Mark?'

'No tools and no time. Those Indians must still be around here for him to have been still alive. Probably they were too busy chasing his horse to worry about him. Our duty is to warn the train. Move softly now and keep your eyes open. Ride!'

They headed for the south and sent their mounts loping over the sparse grasslands. Mark rode with an easy grace and even Skip, sore as he was, managed to hold his seat without too much trouble. They galloped up a slope, down into a valley, up a slope again and then eased their reins as their mounts increased their speed. Mark set the pace and, looking behind him, Skip could tell why.

From the summit of the wooded slopes behind them, a tall, thin, wavering column of smoke rose silently into the heavy air.

5

The next two weeks were a time of terror. Always the wagon train pressed on in a desperate hurry to reach the safety of Fort Deacon and always, riding beside them like a watchful ghost, the thin column of smoke mounted towards the skies. It worried Mark, that smoke. He knew that the Indians must know of the wagon train and he couldn't understand why they hadn't attacked. He learned the reason when they reached the fort.

Fort Deacon, like most of the frontier forts, was stoutly constructed of thick timbers caulked with dried mud and pierced with loopholes high above the ground from which the defenders could fire at any attackers there might be. The walls were high, the compound was large, and the fort self-contained against Indian attack.

The wagon train camped in the shadow of the walls, and Mark, together with Walt, reported in to the Commander.

Commander Breslau was a man who had grown old on the frontier. He listened to Mark and then nodded.

'We had word that Chief Crazy Horse was raiding and I sent patrols to harry their villages. We must have kept them so busy that they had no time to attack you. Unfortunately I can't guarantee that that state of affairs will last. My advice is that you remain here until we have quelled the uprising and then return to Freeguard.'

'Return!' Walt shook his head. 'No. We're heading for California and by hokey we're going to get there. I don't aim to waste much time here, either.'

'Take it easy now, Walt!' snapped Mark. 'The Commander knows what he's talking about. If you set off now it would be suicide.' He looked at Breslau. 'How bad is it, sir?'

'Pretty bad,' admitted the Commander. 'Crazy Horse has managed to unite the Apaches and is remarkably cunning in his methods of attack. We hope to sign a new treaty with him soon, but we can't do that until we've managed to teach him a lesson. At the moment it's impossible to say when that will be.'

'Can't you let me have some soldiers as an escort?' Walt looked hopefully at the Commander. 'Every day we spend on the road makes it that much harder for us to stake a good claim. Give us an escort and I'll start tomorrow.'

'Sorry. I haven't a man to spare.'

'So you say,' sneered the young man. 'Hell, I've heard of you Army men. Sit in a fort all the time and when the taxpayers want some help you refuse to give it. If you'd done your job properly in the first place there wouldn't be any Indians for us to worry about.'

'That will be all, sir.' Breslau looked coldly at the young man. 'I cannot prevent you from disregarding my advice, but I can prevent you from wasting the lives of my men in a futile effort to help you. As things are, the fort is devoid of troops. I wish you good day, sir.'

Walt flushed then marched out of the office into the compound. Mark, about to follow him, was arrested by a touch on his arm.

'Not you, Mr Young, Or should it be Captain Young?'

'I lost my rank when the South lost its army, sir,' said Mark evenly. 'Don't let that young fool disturb you. Fortunately there are other, older, heads in the wagon train. I think that we can make him see sense.'

'I hope so. I would like your company at dinner tonight. Bring some friends with you, not, I may add, our hot-headed young man. I don't think I could relish my food while in his company.'

Mark smiled and followed Walt out to the wagons. Blake came up to him, his face serious.

'Walt tells me we aren't going to get any soldiers.'

'That's right.'

'What's going to happen, Mark?'

'Didn't Walt tell you that too?'

'Walt's a young fool, but even at that what he says makes some sort of sense. We can't afford to stay here for long, Mark. We've got to make a dash for it while we have supplies and enthusiasm for the trip. Once we slow down and stop we may never get started again.' He rubbed at his chin. 'Henderson and I was hoping that maybe you could suggest something.'

'I can suggest this,' said Mark shortly. 'If you're set on going then no one can stop you. But before you go fix up the train properly. Get the men to unship the wheels and grease the hubs. Caulk the water barrels and lighten the loads as much as you can. Strip down and get ready for the hardest and fastest trip you've ever made. Do that and I'll come with you. Refuse to do it and I stay behind.' He smiled at the worried face of the old man. 'The Commander has invited me to dinner tonight. I figured that maybe you and Blake would like to come.'

'Thanks, and Shelia?'

'Why not?'

'I'll ask her,' said Henderson. 'Now I'm going to talk to the others and see that the wagons are made ready. Walt's hot-headed, but he'll listen to reason. See you later.'

Leaving Henderson, Mark made his way to the Marvin wagon and smiled at the pert face of Mary as he climbed aboard.

'Hello, Mary. How's the invalid?'

'Fighting fit.' The gambler, his face pale but his eyes clear of fever, grinned up from his bed. 'Hell, Mark, I'd thought that you'd forgotten me. What's doing?'

Quickly Mark told him the news.

'Walt's right,' said the gambler quietly. 'I've been listening and talking to the people while you were out scouting, Mark, and they really are

95

desperate. They've sunk all that they own in this venture and, unless they can find a place to settle or reach the goldfields and grab a rich stake, they've got nothing to look forward to. I know that the youngster is a hot-head, but he means well.'

'I know that too,' said Mark evenly. 'But facts are facts. The Indians are on the warpath, we've a long way to go, and this is a bad time to try and do what they're doing. Unless they make good speed winter will be here before they get over the mountains, and you know what that means.' He hesitated. 'I've offered to go with them if they tighten up the train. That means that you'll be left behind, Dancer. Sorry, but you're in no state to travel much further. You're lucky to still be alive.'

'I know it.' The gambler winced as he moved, and pain stabbed at him from his wound. 'I'll rest up and join the next train heading west.' He hesitated. 'Anyone else staying behind?'

'The Marvins. Without a fit man

behind them they haven't a hope. As it is, their team is all to hell and the oxen won't last more than a few miles. Gerard will have to drop out too. His wife's expecting and no woman in her condition could make it.' He grinned down at the sick man. 'You don't seem disappointed at the news, Dancer. Would it be that you've plans of your own as regards the Marvin girl?'

'She's a nice girl,' said the gambler seriously. 'Too nice for me.'

'Maybe she doesn't think so.' Mark turned towards the rear of the wagon. 'A man could do a lot worse than team up with a girl like her, Dancer. Think it over.'

He was smiling as he dropped from the wagon. Mary, about to enter, stopped and stared at him. He winked at her.

'My friend's a pretty sick man still, Mary. He may be inclined to rave a little. I mean, just supposing he asked you to marry him, would you?'

Her blush gave him his answer and

his grin widened as he walked away from the wagon. Walt called to him as he passed.

'Mark. You think that there's a chance the Commander will give us an escort?'

'No.'

'Then we're going to try it alone.' He wiped his face with the back of his hand, leaving a long smear of axle grease over his features. 'We're well-armed and can take care of ourselves. What do you advise as regards gear we should take with us and stuff we can throw out?'

'Take water, as many barrels as you can carry. Feed for the animals, ammunition, rope, wheelchains, tools and spare wheels. Get rid of furniture and things like that. Cut down the loads and weed out the poor oxen. If a wagon can't get ready or won't cut down, then make them stay behind. We've got to race against time, Indians, and luck. If we follow the usual route we'll be attacked for sure, but I know another which may get us through.'

'A short cut?'

'No. It will take longer, but it's safer. You want to try it?'

'We can't stay here,' said Walt grimly. 'You're the guide.'

'Fair enough. Seen Shelia lately?'

'With her father.' Walt seemed as though he wanted to say something else, but a man called to him from where he stood by an unshipped wheel, and Mark walked away.

For the rest of the day he helped the settlers prepare their wagons and adjust their loads. The bulk of what they discarded they traded with those who were staying behind, swapping furniture for water barrels, bedding for sacks of feed. The remaining settlers would in turn exchange these items for other supplies and join the next train coming from Freeguard. None of those electing to remain were interested in reaching the goldfields. All they wanted was to find some fertile land to settle and farm and, with the West wide open, that should be a simple thing to do. It was merely a matter of waiting until the Indian menace had been removed, then heading north to the rich valleys waiting for occupation. Only the trains heading due west had to cross the desert and, for them, to avoid the sandy wastes meant a two-month detour and an increased journey over the mountains.

With the bright lure of newly-discovered gold ahead of them such a detour was unthinkable.

Commander Breslau spoke about it after dinner that evening.

'We get all sorts coming through here,' he said. 'At one time I remember this outpost was really isolated, but now that Freeguard has turned into a proper township, it won't be long before Fort Deacon is replaced by another such town.' He sighed. 'So it goes on, gentlemen. Town after town springing up and pushing the frontier further and further back. Next they'll be building a railroad across the continent and then we'll see the last of wagon trains.'

'That won't be for a long time yet,' protested Henderson. Breslau shrugged.

'Not as long as you seem to think, Mr Henderson. Wells Fargo have already established a chain of post-houses across the continent. It can only be a matter of a few years before the railroads push after them.'

'But what about the Indians?' asked Shelia. 'How can they build a railroad while at any moment a war party may sweep down from the hills and attack them?'

'The Indians will be in reservations by then,' said Breslau. 'The Government has granted them a wide expanse of territory on the understanding that we will feed and support them until they become self-sufficient. In return they will leave their hunting grounds and bury their hatchets. The Indian wars will be a thing of the past and the entire West will be ready for development.'

'And the Indians?' Blake looked shrewdly at the Commander. 'Do they agree to move into reservations and give up the lands where they have lived for centuries?'

'They will have no choice,' said Breslau. 'We are an expanding nation, Mr Blake. The Indians, while admittedly with a high culture of their own, are still, comparatively speaking, in the Stone Age. They must yield to progress.' He looked at Mark.

'Perhaps Captain Young can add something to what I have said.'

'Captain?' Shelia looked surprised. 'I didn't know that you are a Captain?'

'I was a Captain,' he corrected. Breslau smiled.

'The war is over now, Mark, don't be bitter about defeat.' He looked at Shelia. 'Captain Mark Young was extremely well known during those unhappy years of conflict. We even had a name for him. We used to call him the 'Fighting Fury', and he caused us more trouble than any ordinary detachment of cavalry. I've heard it said that General Sherman himself often complained that we did not have him on the side of the North.'

'I didn't know that,' said Shelia. She looked at Mark with fresh interest. 'I thought that you were just an ordinary scout and Indian fighter. Why, if you were a Captain in the Confederate Army then you must have been a gentleman.'

'Captain Young once owned one of the finest plantations in the South,' explained Breslau. 'Before the war he was studying to be a doctor, and immediately volunteered when hostilities broke out. I — ' He paused as he saw the expression on Mark's face. 'I'm sorry, Captain, I had forgotten.'

'Forgotten what?' Shelia was interested. 'What did happen, Mark?'

'We lost,' he said shortly.

'But why didn't you return home? After all, to turn yourself into a scout when you could be — '

'I had no home,' he said harshly. 'When Sherman marched through Georgia he left a trail of destruction behind him which devastated the countryside. He burned Atlanta. My people were slaughtered by deserters from the Northern Army. My estates were taken and I was ruined by the carpetbaggers. I had nothing to stay for, nothing! So I left and came West, where a man can stand on his own feet and breathe clean air for a change.'

'But you kept slaves,' she protested. 'That was what the war was all about.'

'Yes,' he said bitterly. 'We kept slaves. True, slavery is a bad thing, but we weren't given the chance to undo our wrong. And now, are they any better off? Have you seen the freed slaves? They are starving because they have nowhere to go.' He shook his head. 'I'm not arguing about it. The war is over and that's all there is to it. Let's leave it at that.'

'About the Indians,' said Blake uncomfortably. 'What's the situation, Commander?'

'Bad, as I told you. Cochise holds Apache Pass and although technically we are at peace, yet several of his braves have broken the treaty.' Breslau shrugged. 'Or maybe we may have done. The point is that everything is unsettled again.'

'For which you can blame the traders,' said Mark bitterly. 'Winchesters were bad enough, but when they started trading rot gut whiskey they were begging for trouble. Once an Indian gets a stomach-full of firewater then he goes crazy. Get a band of young bucks drunk and they'll sharpen their scalping knives and start raiding just for the hell of it.' He glowered down at his glass. 'I'd like to make those traders drink their own poison. Them and the buffalo hunters. Between them they're making the Indians commit suicide by robbing him of both his reason and his food supply.'

'I know,' said Breslau hopelessly. 'But what can we do? With gold miners pressing in, with hunters and traders and settlers coming from the East and trying to stake a claim in the new land, lands which the Indian firmly believe is his. We must protect the settlers and yet we don't want to exterminate the Indians. The reservations seem to be the only answer.'

'Not the best answer,' replied Mark, grimly. 'Geronimo doesn't seem to think so.'

'Geronimo is operating on the Mexican border,' said Breslau. 'He will surrender eventually. They all will, and then everything can be peaceful again and old soldiers like me can retire.'

The talk changed then to generalities and after a further round of the bottle the Commander rose and bid them good night. On the way back to the wagons, whether by accident or design, Mark couldn't guess, both Blake and Henderson seemed to melt away into the darkness and left him alone with Shelia.

'I'm sorry,' she said abruptly. 'I didn't mean to hurt you.'

'You didn't,' he said. 'The war is over and all I want to do is to forget it ever happened.' He looked at her, her face dimly lit by the moonlight. 'You know, Shelia,' he said suddenly. 'I'd feel a lot happier if you were to stay behind.'

'I can't do that, Mark,' she said gravely. 'I must stay with my folks.'

'Mary is staying behind,' he urged. Shelia smiled.

'With Dancer and her mother. Do you think those two will get married?'

'Mary and Dancer.' Mark shrugged. 'I don't know. If he doesn't ask her then he's a fool and if he does and she accepts him then she's the fool. I suppose that they'll both be foolish together. Dancer will ruin his gambler's hands building a cabin and ploughing the grass. Mary will kill herself with hard work mending and sewing and milking until their children are old enough to help out.' He shrugged again. 'Not much of a future in it either way, is there?'

'That depends on your point of view,' she said softly. 'To me marriage with the man I love and the building of our own home is all the future I'll ever want. That is the future, Mark. Someone has to do it to build a nation where other couples can have their children in peace and safety. We must have the rough time so that they can enjoy the fruits of our labours. What else can Dancer look forward to? A life of gambling in one saloon after another until one day he is accused of cheating and shot down like a mad dog. No, Mark. I think that, if he's wise, he'll marry Mary and settle down.'

'He will,' said Mark. 'And then spend the rest of his life regretting it.'

'Why, Mark? Would you?'

'I don't love Mary.'

'Not with Mary, silly. With some other woman?'

'I don't know,' he said slowly. 'That is one question I can't answer. One, incidentally, which you won't have to answer either.'

'No? Why not?'

'When Walt finds his gold he'll be

rich. Then you can marry him and live in the East.'

'I'm not Walt's property, Mark.'

'He seems to think so, Shelia.'

'Do you?'

He shrugged, not answering, then, when he remained silent, she stamped her foot in disgust and moved rapidly away.

Mark smiled after her in the darkness.

6

Twelve wagons left Fort Deacon on the trail to the West. Each was loaded with full barrels of water and heavy with grain and food for man and beast. Outriders kept careful watch to each side, front and rear, and as they wound their way deeper and deeper into the waterless desert so the need for speed became more and more urgent.

Mark, riding with Skip at his side, ranged for miles in search of Indian signs as well as finding the easiest route for the laden wagons. He rode with easy grace, his grey eyes alert as he scanned the horizon, and as he rode he taught the boy the rudiments of his craft.

'The desert is hard,' he said one day. 'But it can be beaten. Tonight, for instance, we'll ride on during the dark. It'll be cooler then and we can rest during the midday heat. See where the

110

arroyo winds between those bluffs?'

'I see it,' said Skip.

'We'll follow it south for about three miles. Then we swing west again around that mass of rock. From then on we can strike out almost in a straight line. It's pretty flat there and there's a waterhole about two days' journey away.'

He reined his grey stallion and wiped the perspiration from his face and neck.

Silently Skip unhooked his canteen and passed it across. Mark shook his head.

'Save the water, son. We may need it more later on.'

'But you said that there was a waterhole.'

'That's right. There was, but it may have dried up by now. If we're lucky we'll be able to drink all we need. If not, we'll have to save every drop for the oxen. Come on now. We'll ride back and report in to Walt.'

The young wagon boss scowled at Mark as he cantered up to the train.

'A fine guide you're turning out to

be. All we've done so far is to twist and turn like a snake in its own tracks. Isn't there a direct route?'

'You're not on the prairie now,' said Mark shortly. 'The desert is criss-crossed with bluffs and dried water-courses. I've found a decent trail and we should make better time after we cross the arroyo. I suggest we push on tonight and rest up tomorrow. The oxen are suffering from the heat.'

'Travel at night?' Walt looked dubious. Wagon trains, even on the rolling prairies, seldom travelled during the dark. It was too easy to lose the trail, to wreck a wagon in some hidden pothole and, anyway, progress was faster during the day. He looked sharply at the tall man. 'What's your real reason? Indians?'

'Yes.'

'Noticed any parties? Any sign?'

'No.'

'Then why worry?'

'They spotted us going to Fort Deacon. They know we halted there and they know we pulled out. I'd take bets that they're waiting for us in the desert. I don't mind a fight, but when I have one I like to pick my own ground. If we can get on to the flat part we'll be in a better position for defence. If they sweep down on us while we're winding among the rocks or crossing the arroyo then we'll be in trouble for sure.'

'Makes sense,' said Walt shortly. 'But what if they attack at night, anyway? We'd be even worse off then.'

'They won't attack at night,' said Mark. 'Indians never do.'

'How's that, Mark?' Skip looked interested. 'Seems to me that they'd be better off with a night attack.'

'Superstition,' explained Mark. 'An Indian believes that if he's killed at night then his soul won't be able to find its way to the Happy Hunting Grounds. They'll attack at dawn, but they won't attack at night.'

'I've heard a bit different to that,' protested Walt. 'I've heard of wagon trains being attacked at dark.'

'I'm talking about a straight charge,' said Mark. 'They may try a few shots or use a few fire-arrows, but they won't come screaming in for the kill.' He frowned. 'At least, they never have so far. Anyway, the oxen need watering. Let me know what you decide to do.'

'We'll try it your way,' said Walt. Standing in his stirrups he put his fingers into his mouth and whistled a signal. Immediately the wagon train slowed to a halt and men and women jumped down and, with buckets filled from the water barrels, began to water the thirsty oxen. Mark stared at the hustle of activity and nodded with satisfaction. These people were efficient in that they knew what had to be done and how to do it. The early slackness had vanished in the face of real peril.

'Time out for chow,' called Walt. 'Bill, set men to watch. Lefty, you check the oxen. Henry, take a look at the wheels. We want no accidents from now on. Move!'

He stared at Mark as the men bustled

about their tasks.

'You aiming to rest up before nightfall?'

'No. I'll ride out again after chow. I'll leave Skip behind, he knows the route, and take a swing to the south. Don't wait for me to get back before pushing on.' He was turning away when the wagon boss checked him.

'One thing, Mark. I've noticed you and Shelia seem to be getting mighty close lately.'

'So?'

'I aim to marry her when we reach California. I wouldn't take it kindly if you was to try and win her from me.'

'A woman is like a horse,' said Mark coldly. 'She belongs to the man who can hold her.'

'Shelia ain't no horse.'

'You should know.'

'Listen, you,' said Walt tensely. 'I don't like you and never have, but you know your job and that's all right with me. But keep your eyes off my girl. Understand?'

'Maybe.'

'There's no maybe about it.' Anger thinned the young man's lips and his eyes became dangerous. He kneed his mount so that it almost touched the grey stallion, and his hand gripped Mark's arm with surprising strength. 'I've heard all about you, you dirty Reb. Well, you ain't no greycoat now. You ain't no Captain either. You're just a hired scout and don't you forget it. Shelia ain't for the likes of you. I aim to marry her and I'll cut down any man who tries to take her from me.'

'Finished?' Mark didn't raise his voice, but something in his cold grey eyes made the young man uneasy.

'Yeah, I've finished. But don't you forget what I say.'

'Take your hand off me,' hissed Mark evenly. 'Take it off before I shoot it off.' He waited until Walt released his grip. 'Now listen to me. This is no time for us to be arguing. If you want to carry it on any further we'll talk about it later. Now get the oxen fed and on the move again. It'll be dusk soon and we've a long way to go.'

He turned, riding off without another word, but as he went his mouth set in a thin line and there was something almost cruel in his iron expression.

Shelia saw it and, seeing it, changed her mind about speaking to him. Instead, she looked at her father, who had both seen and heard everything which had passed between the two men.

Blake shrugged.

'That Walt!' said Shelia. 'To hear the way he talks anyone would think he owns me.'

'Maybe he thinks so,' said her father slyly. 'Did you tell him you'd marry him when we reached the goldfields?'

'Of course not.'

'Then maybe you'd better tell him that he's riding the wrong horse?' suggested her father.

'Why should I?' She tossed her head and tried to look dignified. Blake looked serious. 'Listen, girl. Me and your Ma have spoiled you since you was born, but it's time you learned a few things. Men like Walt and Mark ain't to be toyed with. Either you want one or the other of them or neither of them. Well, if that's the case you tell them so. I don't want you setting one against the other. Understand?'

He gripped the reins and touched the oxen into movement with his whip. The patient beasts lowed as they took the strain and the heavy wagon jolted forward, moving a little to one side of the wagon immediately ahead to keep out of its dust. Behind the train a column of disturbed sand rose like a smoke cloud, a cloud which could be seen for miles and, turning in his saddle, Mark bit his lips as he stared towards it.

There was nothing he could do about the dust. If it moved at all the train was bound to show signs of its passing, but as he searched the surrounding hills with keen eyes, Mark felt more and more the sensation of other eyes watching. Indians could be all around him, hidden behind rocks, staring at the train and waiting for the right time to strike.

The scout hoped that it wouldn't be soon.

That night found the train still moving, the tired oxen plodding over the cooling sands, the arroyo behind them, and somewhere ahead the hoped-for waterhole. Dawn came and after a few more weary miles Walt ordered camp to be made. Despite the need for haste it was imperative to rest the oxen, and both beasts and men were worn out with the long hours of bone-jarring toil.

Not until the wagons had been strung into a ring-camp, the oxen unharnessed and they, together with the horses fed and watered in the shelter of the wagons, did they think of personal comfort. Only one fire was lit to boil coffee and cook a stew, and even before the meal was eaten most of the men and all the women and children had settled down for sleep.

Mark came riding in and wearily dismounted from his tired horse. He rubbed down the stallion, attended to it, and helped himself to coffee.

He was spooning the last of his stew into his mouth when Walt sat down beside him.

'Any sign?'

'Not that I could see.'

'I've been looking at the oxen,' said the young wagon boss. 'Now that we're in the open I guess we'll rest up all today and tonight and make an early start in the morning.' He paused, obviously waiting for Mark's comments. The scout didn't answer.

'Well?'

'You're the boss, Walt,' said Mark tiredly.

'I know, but I'd take kindly to your opinion.' His earlier hostility seemed to have vanished in the press of his responsibilities towards the wagon train in general. Mark shrugged.

'If the beasts are jaded then you've

no choice. No good making a few miles today and losing it all tomorrow.' He looked at the young man. 'How's the water holding out?'

'Not so good.'

'I see.' Mark blinked his fatigue-reddened eyes. 'You want my advice, then here it is. Rest today and move tonight. Travel all night, the country is flat and you can even have a man guide the lead wagon. Send out horsemen to ride the van. By dawn tomorrow you can rest up all day and all the next night.'

Walt looked worried. 'I don't like this night travel. The men don't like it and neither do the beasts. Why can't we move off as I suggested?'

'After tonight you won't be able to travel during the dark. If you move off now you should reach the waterhole by dawn tomorrow. Better to rest up where there is water than where there isn't.' Mark yawned. 'You asked for my advice and that's it. Take it or leave it. I'm going to get some sleep.'

He left Walt staring into the dying fire.

They moved at sundown. They harnessed the lowing oxen and quietened the yelling children. Then, men on horseback and the old men and women, together with the children in the wagons, they set out towards the setting sun.

It grew cold with the swift, incredible cold of the desert so that men hunched in their mackinaws and women wrapped thick blankets around themselves as they tried to keep warm. The night passed, broken only by the plodding sound of the oxen, the creak of the wagons and the soft thud of horses' hoofs as men rode back and forth as they scouted the country.

It grew rougher toward dawn, great boulders making a straight trail impossible and hidden crevasses threatening to smash wheels or break the legs of the beasts. The pace grew slower and slower until it was scarcely more than a crawl, but still they pushed on while the sky grew slowly bright and the stars began to fade with the coming of the dawn.

Mark rode in about then and found Walt eager for news.

'The waterhole is a few miles further on. Bear a little north until you strike the trail again, you must have left it during the night.' He grinned down at Skip where he sat on the front board of his father's wagon. 'Hi, Skip. How's it going?'

'Not so good.' The boy stared disgustedly at the bowed heads of the oxen. 'Can I ride out with you again today, Mark?'

'Not today, son. You'll be needed to do the chores. Wait until we've loaded with water and are on the move again.' He looked at Walt. 'Ride out with me a piece, Walt.'

The young man nodded and spurred his horse ahead of the wagon train.

'Trouble?'

'Indian signs. Found the ashes of several fires, some still warm. They're watching us, Walt. Be ready for trouble.'

'You think they'll attack?'

'Might, might not, you can never tell with Indians.' Mark stared at the sky. 'No smoke yet, but that don't mean anything. Either they think they're strong enough to take us on alone, or they've sent runners.' He rubbed his hand against the stubble on his chin. 'Main thing is for us to get water. Make camp nearer the waterhole and stand ready. Nothing else we can do that I can think of.'

'Is there water?'

'Yes. I checked and it hasn't run dry.'

'Lucky for us the Indians didn't fill it in,' said Walt feelingly. 'That would have just about finished us.'

'They wouldn't do that,' said Mark. 'Remember they need it as much as we do and to them this is their land and the water their property. Anyway, Indians don't fight like that. They do damage, sure, but mostly they fight for the hell of it. The trouble is that they may decide to teach us a lesson and then, especially if they've got whisky, there's no telling what they might do. Let's hope that they haven't got whisky.'

They made camp and loaded with water. Mark insisted that they do that first before anything else, and all hands turned to unlash the barrels, roll them down to the spring and fill them. Lashing them back took time and effort and it was past mid-day before the job was finally done.

A meal was cooked, guards told off to watch, and the rest of the train grabbed some rest. They were up again at dusk, refreshed and eager for a little enjoyment. Mark, looking like new after a shave and a few hours' rest, sat on the shaft of a wagon and smiled as the men and women danced to the strains of a guitar and harmonica played by a couple of old-timers.

He was still smiling when Shelia sat beside him.

'You dance, Mark?'

'I used to, not now.'

'Why not?' She smiled at him. 'I'm sure that a Southern gentleman wouldn't refuse a lady.'

For a moment he hesitated, then, as the music swelled louder, yielded and extended his arm. Together, they moved to nearer the fire and commenced one of the dances popular along the frontier. Mark was just about ready to enjoy himself when a hand fell on his shoulder and spun him around.

'I told you to stay away from my girl!' Walt, his face flushed with temper, stepped back and doubled his fists. 'You got no right to mess around with a man's intended.'

'Are you?' Mark looked at Shelia. 'Did you tell Walt that you would marry him?'

'No.' She tossed her head and the firelight gleamed from her curls. 'Walt takes a mighty lot for granted, but I'm free and I dance with whom I please.'

'You heard her.' Mark stared at the young man. Walt glowered, then as he saw the way she smiled at the tall scout

126

something ugly came into his face.

'I aim to keep what's mine,' he said thickly. 'You asked for it and by hell you're going to get it! Stand up and fight!'

'Walt!' Shelia stepped in front of him, her face flaming. 'You leave Mark alone. You've no right to act as though I was married to you. We're not even engaged and I don't think we ever will be.'

'So he's turned your head, has he?' Walt sucked in a deep breath. 'I don't reckon much of the sort of snake who'd do a thing like that behind a man's back.' He sneered as he stared at the tall figure before him. 'I guessed that something was happening between you two. I've seen the way he looks at you and you look at him. A Southern gentleman he calls himself! A stinking rebel I call him! A dirty women-stealer and a nogood slaver!'

The music stopped and men moved hastily out of the line of fire. Walt had said the unforgivable and, according to the rough and ready code of the West, there was only one answer Mark could possibly make.

He stood, his face like stone, his hand trembling over the butt of his gun. Despite his anger, he forced himself to be calm and to master the fury mounting with him.

'You talk big,' he said thinly. 'But you're young yet and maybe you ain't quite right in the head.'

'I know what I'm saying,' snapped Walt. 'And I ain't yellow either.'

'You — ' Mark swallowed. He didn't want to fight and he didn't want to kill the young man, but Walt was leaving him no choice. No man who wanted to retain the respect of his fellows could allow such insults to pass unanswered. He stared at the young man.

'Take it back,' he said thickly. 'Take it back or go for your gun!'

'No!' Shelia, terrified now instead of being secretly pleased at the attention she had drawn, flung herself forward and gripped Mark's arm. 'Don't kill him, Mark! Don't kill him!'

'Stand aside.' Without taking his eyes from the other man, Mark raised his voice and called to her father. 'Blake! Take your girl away from here.'

'Come here, Shelia.' Blake, his face white with rage, caught her by the arm and almost threw her towards where her mother was standing beside a wagon. Henderson, his features bleak, steadied her as she almost fell.

'Stop them!' She turned to the old man, her face desperate. 'Bill, don't let them kill each other.'

'I can't stop them,' said Henderson flatly. 'That was shooting talk Walt gave Mark and he can't let it pass. Even at that I've never seen a man so patient. Any other man would have drawn on Walt while he was still talking.' He stared to where the two men faced each other, each falling into the gunfighter's crouch, each with the tip of the fingers of their right hands hovering over the butts of their guns.

'Mark'll kill him,' Henderson said.

'I've seen him in action before. I — '

He grunted, a peculiar expression on his face, then very slowly he fell against the girl and then collapsed to the ground. From his back protruded the feathered shaft of an arrow, and even as Shelia screamed other silent messengers of death winged among them.

The Indians were attacking.

7

For a moment no one moved, then, as a woman shrieked in agony as a steel barb tore into her flesh, the camp dissolved in action.

'Kill those lights!' yelled Mark. 'Throw water on the fire. Attack stations!'

He spun, the long-barrelled Colt leaping to his hand, and as arrows hummed through the air he dived beneath one of the wagons. He crouched, his grey eyes narrowed as he stared into the darkness, while behind him the fire hissed and smoked as someone threw buckets of water on the leaping flames.

With the dying of the fire, darkness closed around them and, protected from the tell-tale glare silhouetting them and making them easy targets, the people of the wagon train moved into their defensive positions. Children were put between the crates and sacks of supplies. The older ones stationed with water buckets in case of fire. The men crouched beneath the wagon, rifles at the ready, and the women, as dangerous as the men when it came to defending their homes, stood by to both shoot or help the wounded.

For a while there was silence, a heavy silence, broken only by the cries of the wounded and the sobbing of those who mourned their dead. A shadow moved towards Mark and he turned as Walt approached.

'Many hurt?'

'Five wounded, one seriously, two dead.' The wagon boss was curt. 'I thought you said they wouldn't attack at night?'

'They aren't. That shower of arrows was just the preliminary. We can expect more fire-arrows too, maybe, but they won't charge until the dawn.' He stared at the young man, his face bleak in the dim starlight. 'Look, Walt, you and me have something to settle. We can do it with guns or we can do it now with words. I can make allowances for a man in love with a girl, but that don't give him no excuse to throw around insults. Well?'

'I've known Shelia most of my life,' said Walt slowly. 'I took it hard when she seemed to favour you and I guess my tongue ran away with me. If I miscalled you I'd take it kindly if you'd forget it.'

It was an apology, the best Mark could hope for, and he knew that the young man would rather be roasted over a slow fire than humble himself further. But there was something more.

'I can forget what you said,' he said slowly. 'But you spoke in public and I figure that you should take it back in the same way. I like Shelia, she's a nice girl, and I reckon that she's got the right to make up her own mind. Us fighting and maybe killing one another isn't going to do either she or us any good. Fighting over a woman is the stupidest sort of fighting there is, unless she's your wife.' He paused, looking at the young man. Walt swallowed, nodded, then held out his hand.

'I'll take it back.'

'Now you're talking sense,' said Mark. He shook the proffered hand. 'We've got too much to do and too far to go to carry a grudge. Let's leave it at that.'

He stared out into the darkness, then suddenly rested his ear against the ground.

'Horses. A dozen or maybe fifteen. A small party having themselves some fun.'

'Can we go out after them?'

'Not if we want to hang on to our scalps,' said Mark dryly. He ducked as something smacked into the wagon and something else hummed viciously over his head. 'Arrows. They can see the canopies in the starlight, but they can't see us. Tell everyone to keep down and we'll be safe enough.'

'I've done that,' said Walt. He looked

up at the stars. 'Still early yet; I'll tell the women to get some sleep.'

Mark nodded and watched the young man move away. He stared again into the darkness, then moving quietly from wagon to wagon made sure that the guards were posted and alert. He gave soft instructions as he passed each man.

'Keep your eyes skinned and don't get trigger-happy. If you see something move don't shoot at it until you're sure it's an Indian. Don't let it get too close either. One of you spell the other for a snatch of sleep, I doubt if there'll be time for any tomorrow.'

The men nodded at him, lying grimly on their stomachs, their rifles resting on the spokes of the wagon wheels. Some chewed calmly on a plug of tobacco, others, younger and more nervous, kept fingering their rifles and straining their eyes into the surrounding darkness. Mark had completed his rounds when he bumped into a small shape.

'Skip! What are you doing up?'

'They killed Pa,' said the youngster in

a dull voice. 'Those dirty Redskins shot him in the back. They didn't give him a chance, Mark. They just shot him while he wasn't looking.'

'That's war, Skip,' said Mark gently. 'I guess you want to get a few in return, is that it?'

'That's it. I want to pay them back for what they did to Ma and me.'

'You'll have your chance tomorrow. Try and get some rest now so that you'll be able to shoot straight.'

'I can't sleep.'

'Then stay with your mother.' Mark dropped his hand on the boy's shoulder. 'Look, Skip, there's something you've got to learn. A man has to take care of his womenfolk. Your Pa's dead and you'll have to take his place now. Go back to your wagon and look after your mother; my guess is that she's got enough on her mind without having to worry about you.'

He watched the boy as he stumbled through the darkness back to his wagon, the new rifle hanging listlessly from his hand and his eyes, though Mark couldn't see them, wet with bitter tears.

Mark sighed. He had seen too much of war to be capable of such emotion at sight of the dead, but even with all the past experience he still hated the abrupt misery which death could bring. He shrugged and stared up at the stars. It was near midnight and still several hours from dawn. Even as he watched one of the stars seemed to move across the sky, to shift, to come hurtling towards him. It struck the ground a few feet away, an arrow bound with flaming scraps of grease-soaked blanket and, even as he watched, others came showering towards the wagons.

In moments two of the bone-dry canopies were alight and painting the scene with ruby tongues of flame.

'Water!' Mark yelled the instruction as he grabbed a bucket. 'Get those fires out! Quick!'

The danger wasn't so much in the fires themselves, though the loss of wagons and supplies could be serious. The immediate danger was that the flames were illuminating the camp and making easy targets of the men and women for the searching arrows of the Indians. Walt staggered up, his face a mass of blood from where an arrow had ripped the side of his head, his arms blackened from smoke and flame.

'We're sitting ducks,' he said. 'They'll burn us out and shoot us down without a struggle unless we do something.'

'I'll do it,' snapped Mark. 'Tell the men not to shoot until they're certain.' He stepped towards the edge of the wagons, ducked and, moving slowly and carefully, headed out into the darkness and the lurking Indians.

It was madness. It was taking more than just a calculated risk, but he knew that something had to be done to halt the shower of fire arrows.

The Indians themselves wouldn't attack the train until it grew light. But while they could have fun shooting from a distance, there was nothing to stop them creating havoc.

Mark wondered which Indian genius had evolved this, to them, utterly novel method of fighting. He stopped wondering as he crawled further from the camp.

Several times he stopped and sniffed at the air. Once he made a wide detour around a looming mass of rock, and once he halted, frozen, as something rattled and slithered away.

Mark had spotted the direction from which the fire-arrows came. He knew the effective range of the Indian bows. He knew too that you couldn't have fire-arrows without having a fire from which to light them. He was looking for that fire.

He found it in a tiny hollow, a handful of glowing coals blown to brighter life by a shadowy shape just out of clear range or vision. Mark paused, staring down at the tiny glow, then his eyes narrowed as he searched for the painted braves who must be somewhere near.

One of them found him before he found them.

A shape suddenly rose before him. A dim something smelling of oil and dirt, and the starlight gleamed from the blade of a swinging tomahawk. Luck saved Mark then, luck and his trained response to danger. He leapt to one side, the heavy knife at his belt springing into his hand and then into the body of the Indian before him. Blood, warm and sticky, gushed over his hand as the dying savage fell into soundless death.

He crouched, waiting, his ears strained as his cold eyes peered through the dimness.

From somewhere in the distance a coyote howled. Another answered it and, resting his ear to the ground, Mark could make out the distant thunder of hoofs. They grew fainter even as he listened, and when he straightened again his eyes were thoughtful.

The Indians were unpredictable. They would fight and then, for no apparent reason, would suddenly ride from the scene of conflict when victory was within their grasp. Perhaps the Indians attacking the train had gone to fetch their friends to join in. Perhaps they had been recalled by their chief because of danger to their village from the patrolling cavalry. Mark didn't know, but somehow he sensed that the majority of the attackers had gone. Softly he stepped towards the tiny fire.

It was guarded by two braves, their painted faces looking like visages of the devil as they crouched in its dim glow. The man he had killed had obviously been their lookout and, even as they saw him, Mark sprang into action.

Twice his Colt thundered, his trained thumb rolling back the hammer so that the two shots sounded as one. Then his heavy boots had scattered the fire, had stamped all life from the coals and, his mission accomplished, he ran back towards the camp.

He slowed down as he approached, calling out his name, and Walt came up to him as he climbed over the shafts.

'Any luck?' His eyes widened at the sight of blood. 'Mark! You hurt bad?'

'Not hurt at all. This blood ain't mine.' Briefly Mark explained what had happened. 'I killed their fire and shot a couple of braves. My guess is that a small party couldn't wait and decided to start action. Probably drunk or crazy with bloodlust. We can expect the real battle at dawn.' He stared around at the grim-faced men. 'Much damage?'

'Two more men wounded and a couple of canopies burned. Nothing to worry about.'

'Good.' Mark glanced up at the wheeling stars. 'Might chance a shielded fire now and boil water and coffee. Won't be much time for either later on.'

He was right.

Dawn came, paling the east and fading the stars, and in the first pearly light the Indians attacked in full strength.

They came like a horde of screaming devils preceded by a shower of arrows, spears and bullets, and the dust from their ponies swirled about the wagons as the defenders fired back as fast as they could operate the lever mechanism of their Winchesters.

Men died beneath that first charge. They gasped out their lives as lead slashed into yielding flesh or screamed with the pain of ripping arrows. The Indians died too, yelling their warcries as they toppled from their ponies, bouncing and rolling to within yards of the defended wagons. For a moment everything was wild confusion, with the crack of rifles mingling with the roar of Colts and the thrum of arrows. Then the charge broke and, in wild retreat, the Indians streamed away from the wagons leaving their dead and wounded behind them. Walt, his face streaked with sweat and blood, gulped water and wiped his mouth with the back of his hand.

'Five dead, Mark. Seven wounded.' His face hardened. 'They got a couple of the women too.'

'That's bad.' Mark thumbed fresh cartridges into the chambers of his revolver. 'See that every man has plenty of ammunition. They'll be back soon.' He looked down as someone tugged at his belt. Skip, his rifle in his hands, looked up at him.

'Where do you want me to stay, Mark?'

'Here,' Mark pulled the boy down behind the shelter of one of the wagons. 'Now, you can see between the wagon-beds and fire as they come towards you. You ever shot at anything on the move before?'

'I've been hunting.'

'Right. Get a warrior in your sights, swing the muzzle to follow him, and squeeze soft and gentle.' Mark grinned. 'Just imagine that you're shooting pigeons or wild geese.'

'I'll aim straight,' promised the boy grimly. 'I aim to get ten of the devils for what they did to Pa.'

'Get one at a time,' advised Mark, 'and don't take chances.' He looked to where the Indians had halted and were assembling for the next charge. 'Get ready, Skip, and stay under cover.'

They came with a rush of pounding hoofs and shrieking war-cries. Mark watched them, his hand on the boy's shoulder, the long-barrelled Colt ready in his right hand. Nearer they came, nearer, their faces streaked and daubed with red and yellow ochre, feathers in their long greasy black hair, their naked torsos smeared with paint. Most of them carried rifles, the new Winchesters used as trade goods and given in exchange for valuable furs. Some carried bows, the powerful bows of wood and horn with which they could send their cruelly-barbed arrows almost a quarter of a mile and kill at over two hundred yards. Most carried a spear, plumed and pennanted, while all had knives and tomahawks looped to their belts.

They charged like a band of demons straight from the lowermost regions of hell.

Still Mark waited, his eyes cold as he calculated the distance between them, while beneath his hand Skip stirred and fingered the trigger of his rifle.

'Hold it, Skip,' said Mark quietly. 'No good wasting lead to shoot holes in the air.' He raised his revolver. 'Ready, son? Now!'

Both weapons roared as one and two painted warriors toppled from their mounts. Then firing broke out from both sides, ragged, erratic, mingling with the shrieks of the Indians and the deep-voiced cursing of the men. Smoke plumed from the guns and fogged the scene with the fumes of black powder, and through that fog of smoke and dust the Indians came riding directly towards the train.

They reached the wagons. They surged their mounts forward and jumped over the shafts, then they were all over the wagons, their knives and tomahawks flashing in the sun as they hacked and stabbed at every white person in sight.

For a moment it seemed that the train would be overwhelmed, then Mark, his face a red mess from a torn ear, took a loaded gun from a dead hand and, standing as coolly as though he were at target practice, shot fast and often towards the red savages. Others followed his example. Men forced themselves to stand aloof and pour a withering fire into the Indians, who, mad with the scent of blood, lost all organisation and purpose as they reverted back to their primitive weapons.

As abruptly as it had come, the charge broke, the Indians milling as they urged their ponies away from the withering fire, but this time, instead of retreating, they began to circle the wagons, riding in a wide ring and shooting a hail of bullets and arrows at the defenders.

'Skip!' Mark stared around him at the ghastly scene of broken and shattered bodies lying on the blood-soaked ground. 'Skip, where are you?'

'I'm all right, Mark.' Skip crawled out from beneath a wagon. He looked sick and his face was strained and white.

'Good. Go and find your Ma.' Automatically Mark reloaded his own pistol and the one he had picked up. He stared around and saw Walt, his left arm impaled by an arrow, staggering towards him.

'Mark! Have you seen Shelia?'

'No.'

'I can't see her,' said Walt desperately. 'I'm afeared she may be dead, or worse.'

'I'll find her.' Mark stared at the crumpled bodies. 'Get some men to throw this carrion outside the wagons. Get the wounded into the wagons and let the women tend them. Order the men to reload after using half their shots, we don't want a sudden charge to catch us when we're low on ammunition.' He ducked as lead whined past his ear. 'And tell everyone to stay under cover.'

'But Shelia.'

'I'll find Shelia.'

Mark found her, pale and white, nursing a man who had been shot through the lungs. Mark stared at him for a moment, then jerked his head towards the girl. Leading her apart he stared back at the wounded man.

'Don't waste no time with him. He's as good as dead.'

'Then that's all the more reason why I should tend him,' she said defiantly. Mark shook his head.

'No, Shelia. Your job is to nurse those who can profit from it. We're under attack, and any man who can pull a trigger is of more value than those who can't. The main job is to get the slightly wounded bandaged up and back in action. The rest can wait, they'll have to wait or we'll all be dead before the day is out.'

Stripping off his buckskins, he plunged his arms into a bucket of water and washed off the dirt and blood. Then he washed his face, his hair and the grime from his broad chest. He was drying himself on his shirt when he saw her expression.

'Don't stand there staring at me, girl. Get me the medical kit and as much whisky as you can find. Tell the women to clear out a wagon for me to use as an operating theatre. Tell Walt to send me in the wounded, the less serious cases first. Get the rest of the women to tearing up sheets and material for bandages. Hurry!'

Grimly he set to work.

8

It wasn't a pleasant job this mending of torn human flesh. Even in a hospital it would have been bad, but here, in the wagon bed with Indians screaming their hate and firing at the besieged pioneers, it was something almost beyond the imagination. Mark sent for Walt first, using Skip as a runner, and the young boss reluctantly obeyed the summons.

'Hell, Mark I can wait. This arrow don't bother me none and there's others need fixing more than me.'

'Maybe.' Mark examined the wound and gently touched the arrow. 'If you think that you'll be able to fight off the Indians lying on your back then I won't bother. But you're losing a lot of blood and unless I can fix that arm you're liable to lose it before we reach California.' Reaching for a bottle of whisky he gave it to the wagon boss.

'Take a swig, this might hurt a trifle.'

'I can take it,' said Walt. 'Hurry, them Indians are liable to charge again at any moment now.'

Mark refused to be rushed. Taking his hunting knife he cut off the feathers of the arrow then, delicately pushing the shaft, he felt for the head, and with a quick motion thrust the severed arrow right through Walt's arm.

The young man stiffened, a hiss of pain escaping from between his lips, then, sweat beading his face, he relaxed.

'I'll just stop the bleeding and then one of the women can tie you up,' said Mark. He picked up the arrow and looked sombrely at the vicious barb. 'War arrow, right enough. These red devils mean business.' He finished plugging the wound and turned the young man over to an elderly woman skilled in the rough frontier necessity of bandaging wounds. 'Who's next?'

A man hobbled in, a bullet in his leg. Mark probed for it, removed it, and wiped his reddened hands. 'Tie him up good and tight.' He passed the man the whisky, the only anaesthetic and antiseptic they had. 'Take a swig and report back to me if the bleeding don't stop. Next?'

'Can we tend to this woman?' said Shelia. 'She's got hurt awful bad.'

'Not yet.'

'But, Mark — '

'Fighting men first,' he snapped. His voice softened. 'Sorry, lady, but you can see how it is. Unless we fix up some men to beat off the Indians we'll all be roasting over a slow fire come sundown.' He glared at Shelia. 'Bring me the next man who needs attention. Hurry, girl! Move!'

She flushed at the sharpness of his tone and silently went to fetch the next patient.

He had a face torn open by a bullet so that his teeth showed through his cheek. Mark washed the wound, pulled out a couple of broken snags, stitched and swabbed the gash, and pushed the half-fainting man over for bandaging.

The next had been struck by a tomahawk and had a flap of skin hanging from his scalp over his eyes. More stitching, swabbing, bandaging. A youth, scarcely more than a boy, had a bad slash on the left forearm. Another had been hit by a spent arrow. A third grinned with pain as Mark dug a bullet from his side.

The procession seemed endless. Almost every man in the camp had some sort of wound, most minor, some severe, a few quite hopeless. Mark didn't even try to do anything for the too badly wounded.

He sweated as he worked, acutely conscious of the screaming sounds of the blood-maddened Indians, the continual snarl of rifle fire and the thrumming smack of arrows as they buried themselves in the stout timbers or found softer targets in living flesh. The interior of the wagon in which he worked began to resemble a slaughterhouse with blood-soaked cut-away clothing, stained swabs and dressings, the gory surgical instruments and red-tinted water.

He paused to take a drink of whisky, letting the raw spirit ease some of the tiredness from his bones, then hitched his gunbelt higher around his waist.

'Next?'

'That's the lot,' said Shelia. Her face was strained and she looked as though she were going to faint. Mark grabbed at a bottle and thrust it towards her.

'Take a drink, girl. Quick!' She hesitated and his eyes grew dangerous. 'Drink, I say. I'm the doctor and I know what's good for you. I don't want you fainting on me, we've too much to do as it is. Now pull yourself together and let's have the women who need attention.'

Fortunately there weren't many of them. Most had been struck by richochets or spent arrows, the thick timbers of the wagons had protected them and the children from serious harm. Mark bandaged various cuts and slashes, removed a painful splinter from a woman's fingernail, then wiped his hands.

'Any more?'

'That woman you refused to see,' said Shelia bitterly. 'She's the last, aside from the dying men.'

'Bring her in.'

'I can't.'

'Why not?' He glared at her, his face grimed and somehow devilish in the softened light of the wagon interior. 'Sick in your stomach again?'

'She's fainted,' said Shelia stiffly. 'I can't lift her.'

'Then why didn't you say so?' Mark jumped down and stared at the woman who lay slumped in the shelter of the wagon. Stooping, he picked her up, cradling her in his arms as though she had been a baby and helped by the other women, carried her into the wagon. Swiftly he examined her, his face grave.

She had been shot, the bullet penetrating low on the left side and, as he stared at the wound, he shook his head.

'Can't you do something for her?' Shelia bit her lips, as the unconscious woman stirred and moaned a little. Mark reached for a canteen and let a thin stream of water trickle between her lips. She moaned again, blinked, then stared up into his face.

'Am I hurt bad, Doc?'

'Pretty bad.' He didn't correct her misuse of the title. She tried to shrug.

'It don't matter anyhow,' she said softly. 'Seth had his skull opened by a hatchet and I lost my boy last year. I guess a woman on her own ain't much loss to anyone.'

'We'll get you well,' said Shelia. 'Pretty soon you'll be up and around and forgetting all this.'

'I don't aim ever to forget Seth,' said the woman. 'He was good to me and he took the hatchet which that red devil aimed at me.' She tried to smile. 'I got him though.'

She sagged, her head rolling to one side and, even as they watched, she died.

In the sudden silence the snapping of shots and the yelling of the Indians sounded somehow remote and far away. Mark sighed, washed his arms and hands, tipped a bucket of water over his head and, still wet, donned his buckskins, strapping his gunbelt around his narrow waist. He checked the loading of the Colt, adjusted the hilt of the knife, and reached for a bottle of whisky. He drank, long, rasping gulps of the potent stuff, and when he finally set down the bottle his face was red and he was breathing heavily.

Shelia followed him as he jumped down from the wagon.

'Proud of yourself?'

'What do you mean?' He didn't look at her, his cold eyes were busy scanning the ring of painted Indians riding around the beleagured train. It was past mid-day, well into the afternoon, and the heavy air was thick with the stench of smoke and blood, sweat and fear. A pony lay a little way out, its legs twisted and a dark hole in its side. An Indian lay near it, his pained face and glazed eyes staring towards the sun, and around him, stretching out to the ring of riding Apaches, the desert was thick with dropped spears, spent arrows, cartridge cases and the silent, twisted bodies of men and ponies.

'You deliberately let that woman die,' said Shelia. 'You refused to see her when you could have done something for her, but instead of that you made her wait until she fainted from loss of blood. A fine doctor you turned out to be,' she said sarcastically. 'Doctor! You should have been a butcher!'

'Listen!' He gripped her shoulders, his fingers digging into her soft flesh with frightening strength and, above his face, his eyes stared with a cold brutality which made her almost afraid of him.

'I'm not a doctor! Do you understand that? I'm not a doctor. What I did in there was butchery, but it was the best I could do. I didn't kill that woman, they killed her.' He released her and pointed towards the Indians. 'You want to blame someone, then blame them. If you think they are undeserving of blame, then accuse yourself for penetrating into this country in the insane urge to find gold. You had a nice home in the East, you didn't have to come out here and neither did that woman. You did and now she's dead. You may die next, we all may die, who are you to blame me or anyone for what is your own doing?'

'You could have saved her,' she repeated stubbornly. She rubbed her shoulders. 'Instead of that you let her die.'

'Don't be such an ignorant fool,' he said harshly. 'We aren't playing games now. I've studied medicine, sure, but not the finest doctors in the world with the finest hospital ever built could have saved her. I know a little about wounds, you had to learn that in order to survive during the war, but that's all I know.' He stared down at his hands. 'If things had been different,' he said softly, 'I might be healing people now instead of having to kill them. A lot of people might be healing others, but the war changed most things and that among them.'

He looked up as Walt came towards them. The young man was pale from loss of blood, and the bandage on his arm was red, but he managed to smile at Shelia and his eyes were unafraid.

'I think that they're getting ready to charge again,' he said. 'They've been slackening off for some time now, riding further out and reducing their fire. I reckon that we stand a chance unless they swamp us.'

'Maybe.' Mark stared towards the distant figures, then narrowed his eyes at what he saw.

'That big chief, Walt. When did he join in?'

'Not long ago. He rode up with a dozen warriors and I thought that he was going to attack. He didn't. He stood off and watched most of the time. You know him?'

'No. Might be Crazy Horse or some other chief.' Mark looked around the camp. 'How we off for water?'

'We'll make out.'

'Ammunition?'

'Not so good.'

'Tell the men to hold their fire. Where's Skip?'

'Under a wagon. He's mighty near burned out the barrel of that rifle of his.' Walt chuckled. 'He's a darn good shot too.'

'Is he hurt?'

'Not a mark on him.'

'Good.' Mark stared thoughtfully around the camp, then back at the Indian he had seen before. The man was a chief, he could tell that from the big war-bonnet and feathered coup stick he carried, and he sat impassively on his pony, a dozen braves around him, watching the attacking Indians. For any Indian to sit idly by while his fellows were attacking was so strange in itself as to be incredible. Mark held out his hand.

'Give me a rifle. I want to try something.'

'The chief?' Walt looked doubtful. 'It's a long way, think you can get him?'

'I can try.' Mark slowly levered a shell into the breech of the Winchester. 'If that is Crazy Horse, then his death will mean the end of the uprising. If it isn't, then it'll be one less Indian to attack us.' He lifted the rifle to his shoulder, gauged the range with an experienced eye, and sent lead whining towards the distant chief.

'Missed.' Walt spat in the sand. 'Hell, he's too far off for accurate shooting, you're only wasting lead.'

'Maybe.' Mark raised the rifle again and took careful aim. As he pressed the trigger a painted brave rode between him and his target. The warrior shrieked, clawed at his chest, then, dying, rode towards the wagon train in a last desperate effort to kill the hated white man. He toppled from his horse before he had covered half the distance.

'Bad luck,' said Walt. 'You aim to try again?'

'I — ' Mark narrowed his eyes as he stared into the distance. 'Look! Smoke signals!'

He pointed, and the others, following his gesture, saw a thin trail of smoke climbing into the cloudless sky. Others followed it until three of the thin plumes mounted towards the heavens. Even as they watched, the smoke became interrupted, rising in fitful puffs as the Indian sending the signal caught the smoke in a blanket and released it at irregular intervals.

'What do they mean?' Walt scowled at the distant smoke. 'More of the red devils coming?'

'I don't know. They've got scouts out and they're signalling for some reason. I can't read smoke, I don't know a white man who can, but it means something to the Indians, look at them!'

The Indians had also seen the signals and they had abruptly broken from their circling of the wagon train. They all clustered together and appeared to be arguing with the big chief. He lifted his coup stick, seemed to say something, then with shocking suddenness the entire band of savages turned and charged straight towards the wagons.

'Hold your fire,' yelled Mark desperately. 'Make every shot count.' He ducked beneath the shelter of a wagon as lead whined towards him. 'Keep down and shoot fast and straight. Hold it! Now!'

Fire snarled from the ring of wagons. From between the thick spokes of the wheels, the edges of the wagon beds, from behind sacks of feed and crates of supplies, men, boys, women, all seized a weapon and triggered lead towards the howling band of painted warriors sweeping down at them. For a moment nothing seemed to happen, then all at once the desert was littered with the bodies of dead and dying men and ponies. Still the Indians advanced, riding directly towards the flaming guns, shooting, hurling their spears and tomahawks, darkening the air with arrows in a last desperate attempt to utterly destroy the little band of pioneers.

The charge reached the edge of the wagons, engulfed it, and the red hell of hand-to-hand fighting replaced the cold butchery of long-distance weapons. Knives flashed and dulled as they drank blood. Tomahawks swung with fanatical frenzy, and the thud of reversed rifles smashing against shaven skulls and painted faces mingled with the roar of Colts and the screams of women.

Horses whinnied and threshed with their hoofs. Indians yelled their war-cries and men cursed as they fought like madmen to beat back the painted warriors. For a moment it seemed as if nothing could save the wagon train from utter destruction, then, as suddenly as they had charged, the Indians had gone.

Mark stared after them, blood welling unnoticed from a gash on his arm, his face blackened and grimed, smeared with Indian blood and the fumes of exploding powder. Walt, a splintered rifle in his hands, joined the tall scout.

'They had us for sure,' he babbled. 'I could even feel their scalping knives lifting my hair, and then they went. Look at them, running away as if we were after them.' He wiped blood from his eyes. 'I don't get it.'

'That charge was their last,' said Mark. 'They've gone now for good.' He stared thoughtfully at the rising columns of smoke. 'I wonder why?'

The answer came in the thin sound of a bugle. It echoed across the desert and, at its sound, women sobbed with relief and men sighed in relaxation.

'The cavalry!' Walt stared at Mark as though he couldn't believe his ears. 'They've sent out the cavalry!'

'That accounts for the smoke. Their scouts must have seen the column and signalled to get the hell away from here. They tried just one last charge and then gave up when we proved too strong for them.' Mark shrugged, looking at the litter of dead. 'Indians! Ten more minutes and they would have had our scalps. Five more minutes and they could have wrecked the train for good. A half an hour and they could have taken what they wanted, stole our guns and ammunition, horses and blankets, collected our scalps and been halfway back to their lodges. No wonder they can never win a war when they fight the way they do.'

'Lucky for us,' said Walt feelingly. He stared at the men around him. 'They done enough damage while they were at it for us not to complain they didn't stay a while longer.'

'Yes,' said Mark tiredly. He thrust his forgotten pistol back into his belt. 'Well, let's get on with tidying up the mess.'

It looked like being a long job.

9

Eight wagons left the waterhole a week later on their way to the western coast. Behind them they left the wreckage of the other four wagons, stripped of everything of value and left to whiten and rot beneath the fierce sun. They left more than just the empty shells of the wagons. They left stone-piled graves and a simple cross in memory of those who had died during the fighting.

Too many had died.

There wasn't a family without cause to mourn. Shelia, her eyes moist with weeping, sat beside her father as he grimly stared over the lowered heads of the oxen. Martha had been killed during the final onslaught and now he felt lost and alone where before he had been eager for the great adventure. In a compact line the wagons rolled across the desert, men groaning as they tossed in wound-induced fever, others nursing their cuts and slashes as the heavy wagons jolted over the winding trail.

Ahead of them rode Mark, Skip at his side. The boy had grown into manhood during the battle, and now rode with an easy assurance, his eyes bitter as he searched the desert for Indian signs. Mark watched him, noting the tenseness of the young body and the tightness of the mouth and the eagerness with which he nursed his rifle. One day as they sat over a small fire waiting for the coffee to boil, the tall scout mentioned what was on his mind.

'You hate all Indians, don't you, Skip?'

'That's right.' Memory darkened the boy's face. 'Red heathens. I'd like to get them over my sights and gun-shoot every one of them.'

'Why?' Mark reached out for the coffee pot and poured two cups full of the fragrant brew.

'Why? You kidding, Mark?'

'No, Skip. This is serious. Why do you hate the Indians so much?'

'They killed Pa, that's why. They killed Mrs Henderson, and Jake and Lefty. You know what they did to us, Mark.'

'Sure I know what they did to us, but do you know what we've done to them?'

'We didn't do nothing. We weren't hurting them just crossing the desert. They could have let us be instead of trying for our scalps.'

'I don't just mean us, Skip. I mean white men in general. Do you?'

'We've dealt fairly with them,' said Skip stubbornly. 'Anyways, they ain't got no right to keep us off our land.'

'Our land, Skip?' Mark shrugged. 'Look, son, I've been watching you, and from what I see you're turning into an Indian-hater. That's bad, Skip. A man loses a lot when he turns into a devil, and that's what anyone who thinks nothing but hate is. I've seen it happen before and I don't want to see it happen again.'

'Talk,' said Skip impatiently. 'Maybe if you'd lost your folks in an Indian raid you'd think twice about liking them so much.'

'I lost my folks to our own kind, Skip,' said Mark quietly. 'They acted worse than any Indians. They shot and slaughtered innocent people and burned down their houses while they were still alive and unable to get out. White men did that, Skip. Deserters from the Northern Army. I've as much right to hate the North as you have to hate the Indians. More. Those white men weren't fighting for their existence as the Indians are. They knew what they were doing and did it just the same.'

'That's different, Mark. You was at war.'

'And the Indian is at war too, Skip.'

'What war? We don't want war with them. Hell, Mark, we offer them land to live on and food and everything. They don't have to act the way they do.'

'No?' Mark sighed and sipped at his coffee. 'Let me tell you something, Skip. The Indians have been here a long time now. They roamed this country before the first settlers came and they think that the land where their fathers lived and died is their land. Can you blame them for that?'

'It's a big country,' said Skip stubbornly. 'They can't expect to hold it all.'

'They didn't. At first they moved back and let us settle in the East. Then, slowly, we began to move towards the West. We settled their land, Skip, claim-jumped them, you might say. So, not liking that, the Indians hit back.'

'And we taught them a lesson,' replied Skip. Despite himself he was interested.

'That's right,' said Mark evenly. 'We had trouble. It didn't last long because we made treaties and swore that we wouldn't take any more land. We broke those treaties, Skip, One after the other we broke them. We kept on taking land they had hunted for generations. We pushed them back, treated them like dirt, shot and killed them, burned their lodges and laughed at their culture. So, after a while, they went on the warpath again.'

'We settled their hash,' said Skip grimly. 'We sure did.'

'Maybe, but look at it this way. If you was an Indian and someone came on to your land and started pushing you around, wouldn't you do something about it?' Mark didn't wait for an answer. 'But the worst part was the buffalo-hunters. The Indians depend on the buffalo, Skip, as we depend on sheep and cattle. More. The buffalo gives them all they need. The hide for their wigwams, meat for food, the sinews for bowstrings and thread, bones for arrows and spears, fat and oil to grease themselves against the mosquitoes and rain. Without the buffalo the Indian can't live. With it he can exist as he has always done.'

Mark stared sombrely into the dying

ashes of the cook-fire.

'I've seen a buffalo hunt, Skip. There used to be great herds of them roaming the prairie, and every so often just before winter the Indians would gather for the hunt. They used to ride among the buffalo and spear them to death. They killed enough to give them meat and hides to last the winter. They used every scrap of the beast and they even collected its droppings to use as fuel. That was a fine sight, Skip. A pity that you will never be able to see it.'

'Why not?' Skip looked truculent. 'Who's going to stop me?'

'There aren't any more buffalo herds, Skip,' said Mark quietly. 'The buffalo hunters moved in with their Sharps rifles and slaughtered them for the sake of their hides. They left the meat to rot and the bones to bleach in the sun. I've seen great stacks of those bones, hundreds of tons of them, and all for the sake of a few dollars profit for the sale of the skins. They didn't worry about the Indians not having anything to live on. They just went ahead and slaughtered the herds. Can you blame the Indians for trying to stop them?'

'You talk like an Indian-lover,' said Skip bitterly. 'All I know is that they killed my Pa.'

'I'm not asking you to love the Indians,' said Mark. 'I'm trying to get you to understand them. They killed your Pa and they killed a lot of other people, but in any war people get killed, Skip. You killed your share of them in the fighting, did you ever stop to think that maybe some Indian boy might feel as you do now?'

'That was self-defence.' Skip didn't sound so sure of himself. 'If I hadn't got them they would have got me.'

'That's right, Skip, but I'm not worried about what's past. I'm trying to get you to see that there's no profit in you hating Indians all your life. Soon, within a couple of years at the most, there won't be any tribes left running round. They'll all be in the reservations. They'll be in there because they won't be able to eat unless they agree to move. With the buffalo dead, the white men moving in and the traders selling whisky and other stuff, the Indians have already lost their way of life. They'll give up and leave their hunting grounds for the reservations. Do you still aim to hate a caged prisoner, Skip?'

'I'd never thought of it like that,' admitted the boy. 'It does seem kind of silly, don't it?'

'I'd say yes.' Mark shrugged. 'I've seen others go that way. Men who've lost a wife or child in some Indian raid and taken to hating the entire race of Redskins. They end up hated by red and white man alike, and, one day, a few of the warriors catch him and put him to death. They don't do it quickly, Skip. They make him last a long, long time. That don't matter. What does matter is that anyone who takes that trail is wasting his life. I don't want to see you waste your life, Skip. You've still got a Ma to take care of and she needs you more now than ever.'

Mark drained the last of his coffee and wiped out the cup. He threw sand over the fire and packed away the cooking utensils. Skip, his face thoughtful, mounted and rode beside the tall scout.

'I reckon Ma will marry up with Mr Henderson,' he said abruptly. 'Will you marry up with Shelia?'

'Maybe.' Mark wasn't surprised at the boy's suggestion that the widow and widower were thinking of marrying each other so soon after losing their respective partners. On the frontier a lone woman had little chance. No single woman could do the hard labour necessary to clear land, build a shack, grow food and raise crops for sale. Not even on the goldfields could a woman make out alone unless she took in outside work such as washing or, like Mrs Murphy, opened a restaurant or hotel for young ladies. And there wouldn't be many young ladies in the goldfields. It was both logical and right that a lone woman should look for a husband to provide for her and to protect her and, with the realism of the West, no one would think it at all strange that the recently-bereaved couple should be thinking of uniting their families.

'Shelia likes you,' said Skip frankly. 'She likes Walt too and I reckon that she can't make up her mind which to take. You asked her yet, Mark?'

'No.'

'Walt has. He put the question a couple of nights ago and she put him off. Said that she'd decide after they reached the goldfields.' Skip chuckled. 'They didn't see me. I was under a wagon and was scared to move in case Walt took his belt to me.' He squinted up at Mark. 'You like Walt, Mark?'

'There's nothing wrong with Walt,' said Mark shortly. He spurred his horse and rode forward, his eyes on the trail. For a while they rode in silence, then, pulling up, Mark pointed to where something dark and misty rose from the edge of the desert.

'That's it, Skip. The foothills. We've got to reach them and climb over the mountains before winter catches us. It can get mighty cold up there.' He sat, looking at the distant mountains, then, sighing, he rode ahead to check the trail.

Walt heard the news at the sundown camp. His arm was still bandaged and he showed the strain of forcing the wagon train on when every instinct screamed for him to stop and rest. He nodded when Mark had finished.

'Good. I was beginning to think that this desert went on for ever. Any chance of game up in them mountains?'

'Maybe. Food getting low?'

'Yeah. We lost a stack of supplies during the raid and we've been using what's left in the communal pot.' He licked his cracked lips. 'I could sure use some fresh meat. It wouldn't hurt the rest of us any, either.' He looked down at the tasteless stew he had on his lap. 'Cornflour and beans get tiresome after a while.'

'I'll ride ahead tomorrow,' promised Mark. 'I'll take Skip and see if we can't get some game. How are they taking it?'

'Not so good.' Walt stared around at the silent men and women. Even now more than three weeks after the battle they still hadn't recovered their enthusiasm. Men sat, their heads bowed, their eyes dull as they stared into the fire. Women busied themselves with household tasks, sewing and mending and scolding the children, whom from time to time started a game only to be hushed into silence for the sake of the sick men groaning in the wagons. Blake, his face grave, came over and sat beside them. He pulled a pipe from his pocket, loaded it, and smoked thoughtfully for a while in silence.

'Mark, how far do you reckon it is to the gold-fields?'

'Quite a spell yet. Why?'

'I've been thinking. Maybe it wouldn't be smart to try and make it before winter. The sick men need rest and good food, and from what I hear it's a mighty hard trail over the mountains.' He hesitated. 'What do you figure, Walt?'

'We started out to reach the fields,' said Walt grimly. 'And that's where we're going.'

'Mark?'

'I ain't the boss,' reminded Mark. 'I'll guide you, but what you decide is your business.'

'Something on your mind, Carl?' Walt eased his injured arm. 'You never were keen on getting to the fields in the first place. That's why they made me the wagon boss. Maybe you ought to speak your piece while we've got time to listen.'

'That's what I figured,' said Blake evenly. 'Look, Walt, I ain't no miner, never was. I'm a farmer and that's what I want to stay. Me and Martha was talking and it seemed a good idea for us to grab a piece of land and build a cabin. We can get some burned clean and a crop in so that we can make an early harvest next year.' He pulled at his pipe. 'That's what we were thinking.'

'And Shelia?'

'She stays with us, and Skip, and any as want to.'

'I get it.' Walt scowled at the fire. 'The going's too hard and you want out. Well, I can't stop you. If you want to divide the supplies and head north that's up to you. Me, I'm going over the mountains to the fields.'

'It was just talk,' said Blake quietly. 'I figured that you might see things my way.'

'I want gold,' snapped Walt. 'I don't aim to break dirt all my life. Over them mountains is a chance for a man to make his pile the easy way. Why, I've heard tell that you've only got to dig in a shovel and pick out the nuggets. We'd be crazy to let a chance like that slip by.'

'Maybe,' said Blake. He didn't seem convinced.

'I've heard the same thing four, five times from different people,' said Walt. 'Everyone from the West tells the same story. Gold lying about as thick as stones. River's full of it. Why, they don't use ordinary money there, they use dust. A man pays for a drink with a pinch of dust. There's so much dust they don't know what to do with it all.' He stared at Mark. 'Ain't that the truth, Mark?'

'I wouldn't know,' said the tall scout evenly. 'But I'd like the answers to a couple of questions. These people you spoke to, all those who told you about all that gold, why did they come East?'

'Why not?' Walt looked baffled. 'Why shouldn't they?'

'No reason. I suppose they were all rolling in coin. I mean, they must have taken time out to load up with all that dust you were talking about. Maybe they were going East to retire?'

'No,' admitted Walt slowly. 'They didn't seem to have any gold except a little to show what the assay was.' He stared at Mark. 'What you driving at?'

'Nothing. Only I've heard these tales too and I've heard others at the same time. There's gold, sure, but you can't eat gold.' Mark paused, staring into the fire. 'I reckon it this way. None of you are miners and most of the land must be staked now. A lot of prospectors rode out and travelled light and they would have got there first. The wagon trains arrived late, they couldn't help it, and don't forget that a lot of Easterners would have shipped out around the Horn. So it seems to me that though there might be a mountain of gold over there, there can't be many dirt farmers. Seems too it ain't much good having a bag of gold dust if you've got to pay it all out for a sack of flour.'

'You reckon that we're too late?' Walt spoke as if he didn't want to believe it. Mark shrugged.

'I don't know. I could be wrong, and probably am, but I'd say that Blake has a point in what he's saying. To me a good farm is better than a stretch of rock. You can't live off a mountainside and you can't grow crops if you're too busy looking for gold.' He shrugged again. 'Still, as I told you, I'm acting as scout and guide, not as adviser.'

'We won't know until we get there and see for ourselves,' said Walt. He looked at Blake. 'It ain't that I'm greedy, but I watched my Pa kill himself trying to get a living from farming. I watched my Ma grow old before her time, and she died when I was still knee-high to a pony. It ain't the sort of life I'd ask any woman to share, and — ' He broke off, flushing, as Shelia stepped out of the gloom and sat beside the fire. She looked tired, her dress was stained and torn, and her unbound hair was snarled and soiled. Water was low, too low to be used for washing and other than essentials of life. Mark smiled towards her and held out a mug of coffee.

'You look all in, Shelia. Been nursing the sick again?'

'Someone's got to do it and I haven't any children to worry about.' She took the coffee and sipped listlessly. There were dark circles beneath her eyes and her hands trembled a little as she drank so that the mug made little clicking noises as it rattled against her teeth.

Walt half-moved towards her, his arm lifting as though he wanted to put it around her and comfort her. Mark, sitting back in the shadows, watched him, and his eyes grew thoughtful.

'How are the wounded, Shelia?'

'About the same. I think that Mr Coltin is dying, he can't even sit up to drink now. Jake complains of pains in the stomach and I don't think that Mrs Crew is going to last out the night.' She sighed and put down the mug. 'All this seems so different from what we hoped when we first set out. People we knew, friends of ours, dead and dying and the train cut down to almost half. We were fools ever to have tried it.'

'No,' said Mark gently. 'Not fools. Someone has to do this so that others can follow us.' He rose, tall and slender in the firelight, the flames reflecting from the ivory-coloured butt of the revolver at his side and the hilt of his knife. He smiled down at her, his grey eyes warm with understanding.

'Better turn in now. The earlier we can start, the sooner we'll get off the desert and into the foothills. Things may be easier then.'

Shelia nodded and, accompanied by her father, crossed to her wagon. Mark, after a moment's thought, went on his rounds to check that everything was all right.

He stood for a long time staring out over the desert, and once, when a coyote howled in the distance, he shivered.

10

They reached the foothills with groaning wheels and starving oxen. They crawled slowly towards the hidden summits of the mountains, manhandling the heavy wagons up the slopes and cursing the flies which swarmed around them. They found a creek and a flat, wooded place, and there they stopped to rest the oxen, to overhaul the wagons and to give the wounded a chance to live or die. Behind them, looking remote and distant now, the desert seemed like a bad dream.

Mark roved far and wide in the search for game. He found little, the foothills seemed to have been swept clean of animal life. He shot some birds, a deer, a couple of foxes and once, after a two-day stalk, a small brown bear. It was little, but the fresh meat put new life into the party and, as the days passed, they began to regain their old spirit. Three men died and were buried. The rest of the wounded recovered sufficiently to help out in small tasks and, with greased wheels and rested oxen, they began the long and difficult climb over the mountains.

They followed a trail, hardly visible and often lost. A winding trail which led them past rivers and crags, swampy ground and valleys infested with great horseflies, each an inch long and capable of tormenting a horse or ox to madness. The children rode on the shafts, each with a switch in his hand, and constantly brushed the blood-seeking flies from the necks and backs of the oxen. The outriders, unable to range far in the increasing denseness of the wooded slopes, tied their mounts to the tails of the wagons and took turns at the reins.

As they climbed, the going became more difficult, and imperceptibly it began to grow colder and colder, so that in the early morning their breath plumed from their mouths in vaporous whiteness and all were eager for the hot coffee served from the big pot.

Walt, his face anxious at the slow progress they were making, took Mark to one side.

'Listen, Mark. I don't want to scare the folks, but supplies are getting low. Three more days and we'll be out of coffee. Five more and we'll have used the last of the flour. Can't you find us some game?'

'I'm trying.' Mark stared at the forest around them. He looked bleaker than ever, his face had tightened until his eyes burned from the taut flesh with a coldness seeming to stem from inner fires. Always spare, he had reduced to wire and sinew, utterly devoid of fat. With his sun burned face and hands, his buckskins and weapon belt, he looked the typical pioneer.

'Can't you break a new trail, Mark? The one we're following don't seem to be getting us anywhere.'

'I've ranged the country for twenty

miles,' said Mark curtly. 'This is the only trail. It leads to the single pass in this vicinity. If we leave it we'll get lost for certain.' He rubbed at his chin. 'What I can't understand is the absence of game. It happens sometimes. Somehow, for no apparent reason, the game desert their usual haunts. I don't know why, no one does, but we seem to have arrived at such a time. The last time I was here you couldn't move without flushing a flock of birds or bumping into a herd of deer. There was bear too, and other life, plenty to live on for a year or more. The Indians used to trap around here and they always had plenty of furs for trade.'

'That don't help us none,' snarled Walt. He squinted up towards the sky. 'Looks as if it might be getting ready to snow up there.'

'Might,' agreed Mark. He swung into his saddle. 'I'll see what I can find. In the meantime you keep to the trail and make what speed you can. Get some men on ropes to help out the oxen in the steep places. Have everyone walk who is able. We start climbing fast in a mile or so.'

Walt nodded.

Slowly the wagon train climbed from the foothills towards the summit. The flies had gone, the cold had prevented them from following the train, and the trail now wound through tall conifers, their big wheels sinking into the soft, needle-covered ground. Men sweated as they hauled on long ropes attached to the heavy wagons. Pulling and straining, they relieved the oxen of some of the burden, tugging the heavy wagons up steep slopes and over hidden rocks with sheer muscle and energy. Beside the wagons walked the women and children, the older ones ranging wide in a search for edible roots or small game. Sometimes they were lucky and the cooking-pot steamed to rich food. More often they were not, and then they ate a tasteless gruel of watered-down flour mixed with a handful of dried beans and strengthened with tree bark.

Upwards they climbed, higher and higher towards the snowline and the single pass which led across the mountains and down towards the rich and fertile plains of California.

Then one morning they woke to find it was snowing.

Mark, bundled in his mackinaw, gulped at the hot mixture of herbs and leaves which had replaced the used-up coffee. He had been riding all night, sleeping in the shelter of a crag, and finding his way by star and moonlight. He had rejoined the train just before dawn.

'We should reach the pass by tonight,' he told Walt. 'So far we're lucky, we can get through it without too much trouble, but if this snow keeps up we'll be buried in and have to winter up here.'

'Or go back,' said Walt grimly. He stared down the wooded slopes up which they had struggled with so much effort. 'I don't hanker on going back down after all this work. We've got to get through that pass.'

'We can try,' said Mark. He sipped at the hot liquid. 'I've scouted down a little way on the other side. It's pretty steep, you'll have to lock wheels and rope down, but you can make it. I didn't see much sign of game, but I didn't expect to. We're too high here for anything but a few birds and maybe a bear.' He finished the last of the hot drink. 'Well, let's get moving.'

If progress had been slow before, it was almost a crawl now. The wagons sunk to their axles in the snow and had to be heaved out with brute force. Mark helped, bending his strength to the ropes and, as the going got worse, everyone, men, women and children, hauled at the lines and dug away the snow clogging the wheels. By mid-day they had covered maybe two miles, and the entire band were exhausted.

'We'll have to do it the slow way,' said Mark. 'Hitch up extra oxen to one wagon, drag it over the pass, and then come back for another. We'll kill ourselves and the beasts trying it this way.'

It was a slower method, but it worked. With four teams of oxen pulling a wagon and everyone helping to clear the path, they managed to get two wagons over the pass before nightfall.

The next morning they took the patient animals back through the snow and fetched two more. Three days later they had crossed the pass and shivered in camp while the winds mounted and the heavens unloosed a blizzard which closed the pass until the spring.

They had only just managed to cross in time.

But their troubles were far from over. Snow covered everything and now, for the first time since setting out, they experienced the pangs of actual starvation. Men grumbled as they sweated in the freezing temperature, locking the wheels of the wagons and leading the oxen through the slippery carpet. The first part of the descent was even slower than the ascent and, blinded by the wind-borne snow, hunger-cramps gnawing at their stomachs and the unending labour of easing the wagons down the slopes sapping their morale, they were ripe for trouble.

'We got grain,' said one man savagely. 'We can eat if we've a mind to. What's the point of starving when we've got seed?'

'We'll need that seed,' said Blake. 'What you aim to plant with when we arrive if you eat it?'

'We ain't gonna plant,' said the man. 'Not with all that gold lying around. Hell, we'll be too busy getting rich to worry about a few lousy bags of seed. I say we eat it.'

'Wait!' Mark glowered at them, his harsh face savage. 'You can eat that seed, sure, and then what? Hell, the little we carry ain't going to make all that difference. If we was starving I'd say eat it, seed's no good to a dead man, but we're a long way from starving. We've got leather, there's bark on the trees, and every step we take leads us down into the places where we can find game. Eat that seed and you'll have nothing when you arrive. Save it and maybe you can stake out a couple of farms while you dig for gold. Now, get moving, time to whine is when you're really hurt, not just because you've missed a meal.'

They grumbled beneath the lash of his voice, but they obeyed. Farmers all, they knew the value of seed. With it they could wrest a living from almost anywhere in the country, without it they were just beggars hoping to find an El Dorado.

Grimly they continued their fight against the elements.

Four oxen had been shot before they reached the lower snowline. Four oxen dead, killed for food and because they were too weak to progress further. One wagon was abandoned, its wood used for fuel to beat off the mountain cold, and the rest of the oxen looked more like walking skeletons than living animals.

Then they reached sparse grass and tall conifers. There they rested while the emaciated animals regained their strength and, while resting there, they found the cabin.

It was a box-like shack made of thin logs with a stone and mud chimney. Mark found it and, with Walt and Blake by his side, he walked up to the sagging door. He reached it just as it opened and a bearded man, a rifle in his hands, stepped out.

For a moment they looked at each other, then with a cry the man turned and called into the cabin.

'Emily! People! Real people! We're saved!'

A woman came out of the shack. She was pale as though from a long illness, and her hair hung untidily about her face. She stared at the man, then suddenly she fell to her knees and began sobbing out her thanks.

Their story was soon told.

'We was heading for the goldfields,'

said the man. 'Me and some kinfolk of mine. We crossed the desert and, in the foothills, the rest decided to head north and break new ground. They tried to get me to go with them, but I knew better. I went at it alone and made it. That was a few months ago in the summer, and the pass was wide open. Well, I got to the goldfields.'

'Is it true?' said Walt excitedly. 'About the gold, I mean. Is it there?'

'It's there, all right,' said the man bitterly. 'I don't doubt but there's tons of the yellow stuff lying around.'

'Good.' Walt smiled at Mark and Blake. 'I knew it.' He stared impatiently at the stranger. 'Well?'

'You want to know all about it? Well, Mike Johnson's the man to tell you. He's been there.' He looked at the woman. 'Ain't he, Emily?'

'Yes,' he said bitterly. 'We went there. God help us!'

'Why? What's wrong?' Walt was impatient to learn all he could. 'What happened?'

'It's this way,' said Mike. 'We arrived at the fields with what we stood up in and little more. We had trouble getting down, I had to shoot a couple of oxen, they broke legs in holes, and we smashed a wheel. The river ruined our seed and we lost our gear when the wagon overturned in a crossing. But we reached the goldfields and I was all ready to grab myself a claim and start digging up the yellow stuff.' He paused. 'I did too.'

'So?'

'Look, mister,' said Mike patiently. 'I can tell that you're not going to believe what I say. I don't see that I can blame you much. I was the same. I knew it all, and I'd have called any man a liar who'd tried to tell me what I know now. But you're the first people we've seen for a long time, and I'll tell you what happened.' He licked his lips and looked hopeful. 'Anyone got a chaw?'

'Here.' Blake passed him across a plug. 'Help yourself.'

'Thank you kindly.' Mike tore off a

section of the tobacco and wadded it in his cheek. 'Well, it's this way. You can stake a claim all right, but most of the best claims have gone. You can wash a little dust out of the river or dig for it in the hills, that ain't the trouble. The trouble comes when you try to eat.' He made a gesture. 'Everyone's too busy digging gold to worry about growing food. So you have to pay the prices they ask and, believe me, they ask plenty. It didn't take us long to figure out that we was getting nowhere fast. So I sold my claim and bought me a wagon and team. Then I tried to get back across the pass, head north and join up with my kinfolk. I didn't make it.'

'What happened?'

'Avalanche.' Mike looked at Mark. 'Emily and me were lucky to get away with our lives. Even so, she broke a leg. I had to salvage what I could, built this shack, and wait for her to get better.' He wiped his hand across his beard. 'I'm sure glad to see you folks,' he said with simple feeling. 'I wasn't relishing the winter one little bit.'

'I see.' Walt looked at Mark and Blake. He didn't seem to know what to say.

'Can you take us with you?' Mike looked at them with pathetic eagerness. 'I'm a farmer and a good one. I ain't got no tools or seed, but I'll hire out in return for our keep. I'll hire out for three years if you'll help me set up my own farm. I'm a good worker and can handle a plough. I can put up a shack and manage a team. If you take me you won't regret it.'

'We'll take you,' said Blake quickly. 'You can ride with me.' He hesitated. 'You know of any good land this side of the mountains?'

'If you want good land then swing south after you reach bottom,' said Mike. 'The goldfields are north, a fair ways north and the land that way is all claimed. I heard tell that there's unsettled land to the south, good land too, so they told me, and the climate's right for good crops.' He looked wistful.

'Sure wish that I'd swung south when I had the chance.'

Henderson looked doubtful.

'I was figuring on heading north the other side of the pass,' he said. 'I know that there's good land there.'

'The pass'll be blocked until spring,' reminded Mike. 'You got supplies to last the winter?'

'No.'

'Then head south. You can get in a crop and harvest before you know it. You can get two crops a year if you plant right. The land is good and the climate's good, and there's lots of little, well-watered valleys just begging to be settled.' He looked at Mark. 'You look as though you've been around, mister. Maybe you'll tell these folks that I ain't talking for the sake of it.'

'I've heard others say the same,' said Mark evenly. 'It's good land.'

Walt didn't seem to be impressed.

11

Mike and Emily rode with the wagon train when it continued its journey, and Mike proved invaluable with his knowledge of the trail.

'We can make that slope if you lock wheels,' he said at one time. 'There's no rocks to smash the wagons and they'll take it easily.' Or, at another, simpler-appearing descent: 'You'll have to rope them down. There are a lot of rocks and gullies at the bottom and you're liable to get into trouble.'

Roping down was slow, but it was safe. Long ropes were fastened to the wagons and, with a team of oxen taking the strain, the wagons were let gently down the trail. It was Mike who warned them of hidden currents in a placid-seeming river, and showed them the best place for a crossing. He did it without pride, confident with the knowledge which a double trip had given him, and in a surprisingly short while they had reached the foothills and were heading towards open country. At camp that night Blake resumed his discussion as to their future plans.

'I've decided, Walt,' he said, after they had eaten their meal. 'Martha and me are getting married as soon as we can find a preacher. Skip will be coming with us and Mike and Emily. John said that he don't hanker after no gold, and Sam says the same.' He hesitated. 'Looks as if you're about the only one still set on reaching the goldfields, Walt. I'd take it kindly if you should change your mind about it.'

'I've said my piece,' said Walt shortly. 'We agreed to head for the goldfields, and that's where I'm going. If the rest of you have been scared off by what Mike said, that's your business. I can't stop you leaving the train, but I don't have to go with you.'

'I'm sorry to hear you talk like that, Walt,' said Blake slowly. 'I'd figured that you'd want to be where Shelia is.'

'Shelia won't miss me,' said Walt sourly. 'I'm thinking that she don't want me nohow. Maybe you'd better ask Mark what he aims to do.'

'Mark's out hunting,' said Blake. He rose and stretched. 'Well, we've two days yet before we reach the fork. North leads to the goldfields, south to the new lands. I'm aiming to swing south.' He nodded and moved towards his wagon. Shelia, her eyes sparkling, was waiting for him beneath the canopy.

'I heard what you said out there,' she said. 'I don't think you ought to persuade Walt to change his mind because of me.'

'Why not?' He stared at her in the lantern light and his face became grave. 'It's time you was married, Shelia. Walt's a good man and if you don't get him quick you'll lose him to some other woman. If you don't want him, then tell him so. It ain't right to keep a man hanging on a string. That way he don't know whether he's a-coming or going.'

'I told Walt I'd give him his answer when we reached the goldfields,' she said. Blake shrugged.

'We ain't going to reach no goldfields. I've decided to stick to farming and that's what I'm going to do.' He sighed. 'I wish that Walt would join us. Working together we'd be settled in no time at all.'

'So you're trying to use me to get him to change his mind.' She stamped her foot. 'I don't want no man doing what he don't want to do just because he thinks that he can get something out of it. If Walt loved me he wouldn't need to think of what to do. He'd come south with us and court me decent.'

'And Mark?'

'You leave Mark out of this.'

'Sure, but can you? Can Walt? And what about Mark himself? Has he asked you to marry him?'

'No,' she said reluctantly. 'Not yet.'

'You think he will?'

'Why not?' She smiled. 'Am I so ugly

that he wouldn't think of it?'

'Times like this when I wish you was a boy,' he said wearily. 'Sarah might have shaken some sense into you, but I can't. Mark ain't the man for you, girl. You've known Walt all your life and you know how to handle him. Mark is something else. I've seen men like him before. Hard, cold, restless, always on the move and ready for trouble. You think that he'd want a farmer's daughter for a wife?'

'A man has to settle down some time,' she said. 'Mark's a good man, a gentleman. I'd make him a good wife and he'd treat me right.'

'Maybe.' Blake shook his head. 'I don't know. I like Mark and I like Walt. I like Walt a lot better than I did at first. He's stubborn, but that ain't no crime. He loves you and wants to marry you. Mark, he might love you too, but not in the same way.' He took her by the shoulders and stared at her. 'I don't want you to get hurt, Shelia. I don't want you to do anything you might have cause to be sorry for later on. Pick one or the other, but pick as your heart tells you. Mark's a stranger, he's got glamour, and maybe you're attracted to him because of that. But you've known Walt for a long time.' He shook her gently, but firmly. 'Make up your mind, Shelia, and have your answer ready by the time we reach the fork.'

He picked up his bed-roll.

'Reckon I'll sleep in the open tonight. It's getting kind of warm. Good night, girl.'

'Good night, Pa.' Shelia waited until he had gone, and then turning out the lantern undressed and prepared for sleep.

But it was a long time coming.

Mark rode on the wagon during the last day before they reached the fork. His work was over, the trail lay plain before them and his services as guide and scout were no longer required. His horse, the grey stallion, trotted beside the wagon, contentedly pawing the ground and racing ahead to wait for them to catch up, cropping at the grass while he waited.

It was a peaceful scene and, as Mark stared over the yoke of the oxen, his face softened a little and some of the bleak harshness which had been with him during the trek over the mountain left him.

Looking sideways at him from the corners of her eyes Shelia felt the magnetism of him, the sheer masculinity of a man who lived on the thin edge of danger and who had roved far and wide across the vast expanse of the West. She picked up a switch and idly flicked it over the heads of the patient beasts.

'Soon be at the fork, Mark,' she said casually.

'That's right.' He turned and stared at her, appraising her with his frank eyes, and beneath his stare she flushed a little.

'What you aiming to do, Mark?'

'I'm not sure yet. May take a ride up into the goldfields.'

'Oh.' His answer disconcerted her. She bit her lower lip, then, with the frankness of the pioneer, stared full at him.

'Have you ever thought of settling down, Mark?'

'Often.'

'A man could do a lot worse than break new ground, build a cabin and get himself a wife.'

'Like Dancer?'

'Why not? I'll bet he finds a steady home is better than all this moving around. What's it get you, Mark? You own a horse, a gun, the clothes on your back and maybe a little cash. And that's all. If you struck roots you'd have a home and no more wandering. You'd have a place to call your own, children, neighbours and friends. A man needs all those things, Mark. A man ain't a wolf to go wandering around killing Indians, and maybe getting himself shot and left for the vultures. Seems to me that a man would get to learn that for himself.'

'Some men can't settle down,' he said quietly. 'Some men have the urge to see what's on the other side of the hill and then, when they've seen it, they want to have a look over the next one. There's always another hill, Shelia. You know that, don't you?'

'I know it.' She stared at him and now she was no longer blushing. 'You trying to tell me something, Mark?'

'Do I have to?' He smiled at her, and with the smile he seemed to become transfigured so that the hardness and bleakness all vanished and left only the clean features and steady eyes of a young man.

'Maybe not, Mark,' she said slowly. 'But I'd like to hear it just the same.'

'You want me to ask you to marry me,' he said, and his hand fell upon hers and gripped it with affectionate tenderness. 'You're a lovely girl, Shelia, and you'd make any man a wonderful wife, but — '

'But not for you. Is that it, Mark?'

'You're not in love with me, Shelia,'

he said quietly. 'Oh, you may think you are, but way down deep, in the place where it really matters, you're not. I like you too much to ask you to give up all you know and leave your father and friends. No, Shelia. Walt's your man.'

'Supposing I say that he ain't?' She stared at him, wanting him now more than ever with the perversity of a woman who cannot get her own way. 'Supposing I don't aim to marry Walt at all. Would that make a difference?'

'No.'

'You're just like all men,' she said bitterly. 'You think that you know it all. But you don't, Mark. No man does. You like to think that you know what goes on inside of a woman, but when you get down to it you don't. How do you know that Walt's the man for me? How do you know that you aren't? I'd go anywhere with a man I could love, Mark. I'd ride behind him over them hills you was talking about and it wouldn't make no difference to me if I didn't have no cabin.' She looked at

214

him with her soul in her eyes. 'Mark, can't you see what I'm getting at? Do I have to ask you instead of you asking me?'

'Stop it!' Some of the hardness returned to his features. 'Don't talk like that, girl.' He sucked in a deep breath then slowly exhaled. Fumbling in his pockets he found a broken length of a slim cigar and, lighting it, he blew a thin streamer of smoke towards the lead oxen. She took his hand again and waited until he looked at her.

'Well?'

'It would be easy for a man to marry you,' he said quietly. 'It would be easy for him to say 'yes' and settle down and raise a family and grow crops, but if he did all that with a woman who didn't really care for him, whose heart was already somewhere else with some other man, it wouldn't turn out good for either of them.'

'You're a fool,' she said impatiently. He shook his head.

'You forget something, Shelia. When

Walt and I was getting set to shoot each other just before the Indian raid, you had to make a choice. You couldn't help it, you had to do it even though you didn't know what you were doing. Remember what happened?'

'Maybe.'

'You grabbed me and asked me not to kill Walt. You grabbed me and, for all you knew or cared, he could have drawn then and shot me dead. You wasn't worried about Walt killing me, you was only worried about me killing Walt. You made your choice then, Shelia, though you didn't know it.'

Putting his fingers to his mouth he whistled sharply, and the stallion, pricking up its ears, snorted and rode close beside the wagon. Mark rose and, with a last look at the thoughtful girl, jumped from the wagon on to the horse. Stooping, he picked up his roll from the front of the wagon, slung it behind his saddle and touching his hat, rode to where Walt and Blake rode ahead of the train.

'You owe me a thousand dollars,' he said to Blake. 'Want to pay now or later?'

'I've got the cash, Mark.' Blake pulled a pouch from beneath his shirt and held it out to Mark. The tall scout felt it, tossing the bag in his hand, then spilling out a handful of the gold pieces, thrust them into his pocket and drew shut the leather pouch.

Walt glowered at him, but said nothing.

'You coming with us, Mark?' Blake looked hopeful. Mark shook his head.

'Nope.'

'But — ?' The old man turned in his saddle and stared back towards Shelia. He looked at Mark, a question in his eyes.

'She ain't for me, Blake,' said Mark evenly. 'I'm not that much of a fool to marry up with a girl who's got her heart fixed on someone else.' He looked at Walt. 'Fellow, we've had our quarrels, but I've known mules less stubborn than you. Don't you know that there ain't enough gold in all the world to buy what you're throwing away?'

Walt flushed and said nothing.

'Get back there to her,' said Mark. 'Eat dirt, tell her you love her more than all the yellow metal in California, ask her to marry you and quit wasting your time.' He smiled at the young wagon boss.

'Get moving, Walt. Get moving before I change my mind and ride off with her. Take your chance while you've got it and get some sense into that thick skull of yours.'

He slapped the young man on the shoulder and, for a moment, each stared at the other. Then, grinning, Walt jerked at his reins and rode back towards the wagons. Blake followed him with his eyes.

'Thanks, Mark. I take it real kindly that you should have done that. Shelia's farming stock, and though she won't admit it she won't be happy doing anything else.' He looked at the tall scout. 'What are you aiming to do now?'

'I'm taking a ride north to see what's going on. Then if I get tired of that I may head back towards Freeguard, maybe they can find a use for a man like me.' He hefted the bag of gold and tossed it towards Blake. 'Here, you look after it for me. Buy stock or grain or something.'

'I can't take it, Mark. It's yours.'

'You want me to lose it over the bar of some saloon?' Mark grinned, knowing that the money represented the difference between poverty and plenty for the wagoners. 'Take it, use it, and then one day, when I'm passing by this way, I'll drop in and you can tell me what you've done with it.'

He touched his hat, then, not waiting for the old man to speak, spurred his horse and galloped away.

He didn't look back.

We do hope that you have enjoyed reading this large print book.

Did you know that all of our titles are available for purchase?

We publish a wide range of high quality large print books including:
**Romances, Mysteries, Classics
General Fiction
Non Fiction and Westerns**

Special interest titles available in large print are:
**The Little Oxford Dictionary
Music Book, Song Book
Hymn Book, Service Book**

Also available from us courtesy of Oxford University Press:
**Young Readers' Dictionary
(large print edition)
Young Readers' Thesaurus
(large print edition)**

For further information or a free brochure, please contact us at:
**Ulverscroft Large Print Books Ltd.,
The Green, Bradgate Road, Anstey,
Leicester, LE7 7FU, England.
Tel:** (00 44) **0116 236 4325
Fax:** (00 44) **0116 234 0205**

Riding in the desert, bounty hunter Frank Clooney's horse goes lame and he hitches a ride with the Carver family, using the alias Sam Rafter. But the Carver family only brings trouble: Ned Carver is a tyrant, and his wife sees Clooney as a way to gain freedom for herself and her daughter. Then outlaw Spitter Larch joins them, and if Larch remembers who Sam Rafter really is, Clooney's life won't be worth a plugged nickel!

FACES IN THE DUST

Corba Sunman

Pinkerton detective Ward Loman rode into Coldwater, Texas, hunting down the killer Leo Slattery. But there was trouble on the local range involving Leo's family, headed by Hub Slattery, owner of the HS ranch. In the worsening situation Loman rescues Kate Hesp, and is plunged into a deadly sequence of events with its origins in the war between North and South, involving the disappearance of a gold shipment. As Loman expected, gunsmoke and death would be the outcome.

CLEARWATER JUSTICE

Scott Connor

For five years Deputy Jim Lawson had wanted to find his brother Benny's murderer. So when suspect Tyler Coleman rides into Clearwater, Jim slaps him in jail. But the outlaw Luther Wade arrives, threatening to break Tyler out of jail. Then Jim's investigation unexpectedly links Benny's murder to the disappearance of Zelma Hayden, the woman he had once hoped to marry. Can Jim uncover the truth before the many guns lining up against him deliver their own justice?

BLOOD KIN

Ben Nicholas

Cole Vallantry, outnumbered and cornered, desperately swinging punches, is about ready to concede defeat — and not only regarding the brawl in the Buscadero saloon. His mission, the manhunt which had dragged him across Arizona in the blazing midsummer, is at a standstill, the trail having finally petered out. Then a tall stranger wades into the fracas, unbelievably taking Vallantry's side — but what is *his* agenda?

BOUNTY HUNTER'S REVENGE

Ron Watkins

With two years in jail behind him, Adam Milton rode into Cotterton in search of a job. Finding work as bodyguard to Miss Chambers, owner of the Big C ranch, Milton is dragged into the feud between her and ranch owner Trimble. But when Miss Chambers is shot he unhesitatingly steps into the vendetta between the two ranches. The ensuing violence leaves a trail of corpses and poses the question: will Milton become one of them?

DEAD BY SUNDOWN

I. J. Parnham

After five years Mike Donohue tracks down his wife's killer, Galen Benitez, to the region known as the Cauldron. Here, Mike meets Lucy Reynolds who is searching for the lost city of Entoro, rumoured to have streets of gold. As Mike suspects that Galen might also be there treasure seeking, he helps her. Up against Galen, and now Lucy's deadly jealous admirer, Mike will need his six-shooter to ensure that he isn't the one who is dead by sundown.